THE END OF THE RAINBOW

When the attractive Waldo van der Graaf rescued Olympia from a life of comparative drudgery and offered to marry her it was to be a match of convenience. Olympia wanted to escape from her domineering aunt and Waldo needed someone to run his home and look after his small daughter. Could there be anything more to the marriage?

Books you will enjoy
by BETTY NEELS

CRUISE TO A WEDDING
When Loveday heard that her friend
Rimada had a stern guardian who
objected to her wedding plans it seemed
only natural to sympathize and offer
practical help in getting round the
problem. But Loveday was to find that
Adam was harder to organize than she had
imagined!

THE MAGIC OF LIVING
When Arabella was involved in a road
crash in Holland, it seemed providential
that the first person to arrive on the scene
should be Doctor Gideon van der Vorst.
But as she became more and more involved
with the doctor, Arabella began to wonder
if providence had, after all, known what
it was doing!

THE GEMEL RING
'I hope you will believe me when I say
that I dislike you more than anyone else
I know,' Charity Dawson told that
annoying Dutchman Everard van Tijlen.
Perhaps it was just as well that he didn't
take her words too seriously!

ENCHANTING SAMANTHA
Samantha sympathized with the problems
of the elderly Dutch woman who was
admitted to the hospital where she
worked. But she didn't realize that her
encounter with Juffrouw Boot's employer,
the striking Giles ter Ossel, would bring
her so much heart-searching. Perhaps
one shouldn't get involved with one's
patients? Yet . . .

THE END OF THE RAINBOW

by

BETTY NEELS

MILLS & BOON LIMITED
17-19 FOLEY STREET
LONDON W1A 1DR

First published 1974
This edition 1974

© Betty Neels 1974

ISBN 0 263 71717 8

Made and printed in Great Britain by
Cox & Wyman Ltd, London, Reading
and Fakenham

CHAPTER ONE

A SNEERING March wind was blowing down Primrose Hill Road, driving everyone and everything before it, but there was one battling figure struggling into its teeth – a young woman, hurrying along at a great rate, her head bent, her hair, whipped out of her head-scarf, blowing around her face. Presently she turned down a side road and pausing only to tuck her hair away out of her eyes, hurried on, faster now in its comparative shelter. It was a pleasant enough street, lined with tall, late-Victorian houses, nicely maintained still, each with its narrow railed-off area steps leading to a basement, and each, too, with its heavy front door, bearing an impressive brass knocker. Half-way along these superior dwellings the girl stopped, darted up the steps, put down the basket which she was carrying, opened the door with some difficulty, whisked up the basket and went inside.

The hall she entered was chilly and rather dim, with a polished linoleum floor and a table, flanked by two chairs, against one wall. There was a handsome vase on the table, empty, and a scrupulously clean ashtray. The stairs were covered with lino too, and although everything was spotlessly clean and free from dust, it held neither warmth nor welcome. The girl paused only long enough to close the door behind her before crossing the hall and making her way down the stairs beyond a small archway at the back. She had reached the bottom and had her hand on a door in the narrow dark passage beyond when she was halted by a voice. It called sharply from the floor above: 'Olympia, come here at once!'

The girl put her basket down and went upstairs again, opened one of the massive mahogany doors in the hall, shut it quietly behind her, and waited near it, looking across the carpeted floor to where her aunt sat at her desk. Miss Maria Randle was a large woman, approaching middle-age but still handsome despite her severe expression. She looked up briefly now. 'You have been gone a long time,' she observed coldly.

'There was a good deal of shopping . . .'

'Nonsense – when I was a girl of your age, I thought nothing of twice the amount I ask you to do.' She sighed, 'But there, you are hardly capable of a normal girl's work; if I had known when I adopted you, gave you a good home and educated you at such expense, that you would repay me in such an ungrateful fashion, I would have thought twice about it.'

Olympia had heard it all before; she sighed soundlessly, and her face took on the wooden expression which concealed her hurt feelings and which her aunt referred to as mulish. It was a pleasant face, although it had no startling good looks; grey eyes, nicely fringed, a short straight nose, a wide, softly curved mouth and a determined chin didn't quite add up to prettiness. Her hair was a warm brown, hanging round her shoulders rather untidily; it caught Miss Randle's annoyed eye and enabled her to voice another grievance. 'And your hair!' she declared severely. 'Surely you can do something about it? You're a disgrace – if any of the doctors were to see you like this I'm sure I don't know what they would think.'

Olympia said nothing at all; she was perfectly well aware that her aunt knew as well as she did that the

6

doctors only saw her when she was in uniform, her hair smoothed back into a neat bun under a plain cap. Maybe her aunt remembered this too, for she didn't pursue the matter further, but: 'You are on duty in ten minutes – leave the shopping in the kitchen, and see that you're not late. You must try and remember that my staff are expected to be punctual, and that includes you, Olympia.' She frowned heavily. 'Such a ridiculous name,' she added crossly.

Again Olympia said nothing; she rather liked her name, although she was aware that her appearance hardly justified it. She should, she had always felt, have been a voluptuous blonde, and strikingly beautiful, instead of which she was a little on the short side and thin with it, her features were pleasantly ordinary and her hair, soft and long though it was, and tending to curl nicely at the ends when it was given the chance, was usually too severely dressed. But her parents were not to have known that when she was born – probably she had been a very pretty baby, and since they had both died in a motor accident before she could toddle, they had never known how wrong they were.

She went quietly from the room, took the shopping to the kitchen where she handed it over to Mrs. Blair, the hard-worked daily cook, and returned to her room to change into uniform.

The room was like the hall, bare and clean and chilly. She shivered a little as she took off her things, donned the blue dress and white apron, fastened the blue petersham belt round her little waist, and finally smoothed her hair into its demure bun under her cap. She had a couple of minutes to spare still before she needed to go on duty, and the thought crossed her mind that a cup of coffee would be nice; but Mrs. Blair was already cross; by the time she could coax her into giving her a cup it would be too late. She tied the laces of the sensible black shoes her aunt insisted upon and went back upstairs.

The nursing home catered for twenty patients, and it was always full; a number of the rooms held three beds, in some cases two, and on the first floor there were three single-bedded rooms, commanding high fees for that very reason, and usually inhabited by wealthy patients who demanded a great deal of attention, and because they could pay, usually got it, however trivial.

Olympia passed these three doors now and entered a small cupboard of a room where a middle-aged woman in nurse's uniform was sitting. She looked up as Olympia went in and smiled. 'I've just made a pot of tea,' she greeted her. 'I bet you had to spend your off duty shopping,' and at Olympia's nod: 'I thought as much – and now you're on duty until eight o'clock this evening.' She produced two mugs. 'It's really too bad; if I didn't need the money so badly and live almost on the doorstep, I'd be tempted to try my luck somewhere else in protest, but much good that would do; you'd get all my work to do as well as your own.'

She spooned sugar into their teas and they sat down side by side at the desk.

'How's Harold?' asked Olympia. Harold was Mrs. Cooper's teenage son, suffering from muscular dystrophy, and the reason why she went out to work – he was the reason why she stayed at the nursing home too, for it was only a few yards from her flat, and because nurses were hard to get, Miss Randle had reluctantly allowed her to work during the hours which suited her.

'He had a bad night,' said his mother, getting to her feet. 'There's nothing to report; they're all much as usual. Doctor Craddock came and changed Mrs. Bright's medicine ... I'll be in at two tomorrow.' She went to the door. 'Mrs. Drew's making beds upstairs, and Miss Snow is getting Mr. Kemp up. So long, dear.'

Left to herself, Olympia read the report, tidied away the tea things and started on her visits to the patients. They were all elderly geriatric cases; her aunt would take nothing else, since more acute nursing would mean more staff and trained nurses at that. As it was, she got by very well with Olympia and Mrs. Cooper, and Mrs. Drew and Miss Snow, who had had no training at all but looked like nurses in their uniforms. During the night she managed with two more nursing aides, good and competent and hard-working, and if anything needed the skill of a trained nurse, why, there was always Olympia to get up and see to things.

The three patients with rooms to themselves were nicely settled for the time being; she climbed the stairs to the floor above, where she gave out the medicines, did a bed bath, made a couple of beds, and then considerably later, climbed the last narrow flight. Here the rooms contained more beds; one held four old ladies, the other three elderly men, and although they were adequately lighted and warm enough, they were entirely bare of pictures or ornaments. The patients here had little money; just enough, with the help of relations who were horrified at the idea of sending their old folk into hospital, for the fees to be paid, leaving little over for spending. Olympia longed to tell them how much better off they would be in a geriatric unit in any of the big hospitals in London; they would have

9

company there, and the telly, as well as the library ladies coming round twice a week and more old ladies and gentlemen to talk to. She went from one to other of them now, stopping to chat, admire knitting, discuss the weather or look at some picture in a paper. She always stopped longer than she should on the top floor, because the poor old things were mostly incapable of getting down the stairs for themselves, and Aunt Maria, although she paid them a daily visit, rarely stopped for more than a few moments. Olympia, tidying beds and listening with half an ear to their occupants, reflected for the hundredth time on the improvements she would bring about if she could take Aunt Maria's place and run the home herself. Not that she liked geriatric nursing; she had loved her three years' training at a large London hospital and she had done well there. She had wanted, above all things, to specialize in surgery, but she had given her word to her aunt before she began her training, and she hadn't broken it, although sorely tempted to do so.

She knew now that Aunt Maria had been quite unscrupulous and totally unfair towards her. True, she had educated her well, bought her sensible, hardwearing clothes which had been agony to wear in the company of her better dressed friends, and instilled into her, over the years, the fact that she must never cease to be grateful to an aunt who had taken her as a toddler and devoted her life to her upbringing. And when, at the age of fifteen or thereabouts, Olympia had expressed a wish to take up nursing, her aunt had agreed readily, at the same time pointing out that Olympia, as a grateful niece, could do no less than hand over the bulk of her salary, when the time came, to an aunt who had spent a great deal of money over the years. Moreover, she had extracted a promise that upon the completion of her training, Olympia should return to the nursing home and work for her aunt at a very modest wage indeed, because, it was made clear to her, she would be living free, and what girl in these days was lucky enough to have a good home where she could live for nothing?

Olympia, at that age, hadn't known much about that; she promised, only asking: 'And may I never go back to hospital? I think I should like to be a surgical nurse, and perhaps in a year or two, when I've trained, I could get a Sister's post.'

Aunt Maria had laughed. 'Why should you wish to leave?' she wanted to know. 'You have a duty to me, you know.'

'Supposing I should want to get married?' Olympia, almost sixteen, had been a romantic.

Her aunt had laughed again, a little unkindly, and had taken her time in replying. 'My dear,' she had said at length, 'I cannot imagine any man wanting to marry you – you aren't the marrying type.' She had picked up her pen to signify the end of the interview. 'But if such an unlikely event should happen, then naturally you may leave.'

And that had been eight years ago now; Olympia had finished school and until she had been old enough to start her training, had helped her aunt in the nursing home, running errands, cooking when Mrs. Blair had a day off, making beds and sorting linen. She had been eighteen when she had left the house near Primrose Hill and gone to live in hospital, and the next three years of her life had been the happiest she had known. She had loved the work and the busy routine; she had made many friends too and had done well; so well that she had been offered the Sister's post she had so much longed for. But Aunt Maria had nipped that in the bud; reminding her of her promise, so that she had gone back to work in the chilly nursing home and was still there, two years later. And because she was paid very little and seldom went out, she met no one at all; the doctors who visited the patients were mostly elderly G.P.s and even the visitors were old, or at least, middle-aged. At first, in hospital, she had cherished dreams of meeting some young man who would wish to marry her and thus solve the future for her, but beyond one or two dates which had never got beyond the first meeting, nothing had happened. Perhaps, as her aunt had pointed out, she wasn't a girl men would want to marry.

She went slowly downstairs presently, to supervise the patients' dinners, then went back upstairs to feed old Mrs. Blake, who could no longer feed herself. The old people were out of their beds by now, sitting round the table; they enjoyed their meals, they broke the monotony of their days. They lingered over their pudding, talking quite animatedly, and after a little while Olympia left Miss Snow to attend to their little wants and get them on to their beds for their afternoon nap, then went downstairs to the dining-room where her aunt was waiting. They lunched quickly with the minimum of conversation, and that pertaining to the running of the home. 'You must go down to Selfridges tomorrow afternoon,' said Miss Randle as she portioned out the steamed pudding. 'I want you to buy some sheets.'

'It's my half-day off,' Olympia reminded her.

'I'm aware of that, but what difference should that make? I imagine you will enjoy going to Oxford Street

– you have no plans.'

'Yes, I had, Aunt Maria. I'm going to the National Gallery – there's an exhibition of paintings I want to see, and I've arranged to meet Sally Grey for tea afterwards.' Sally had been one of her friends at hospital.

Her aunt helped herself to more steamed pudding. 'You can telephone her and tell her that you will meet her on another day,' she said positively. 'As for the National Gallery, there is always some exhibition or other being held there; you can see something else later on.'

Olympia forbore from commenting upon this remark, for she knew that it would be useless; instead she asked reasonably: 'Perhaps you could go to Selfridges? Mrs. Cooper will be on duty . . .'

Her aunt eyed her coldly. 'When I want your advice as to what I should and should not do, Olympia, I will ask for it. You will be good enough to go to Selfridges. And by the way, I have Mr. Gibson coming to supper and we shall have a great deal to discuss about the next church bazaar, so be sure that you are back here in good time – not later than six – that will leave me free to entertain him.'

Olympia said: 'Yes, Aunt,' in a wooden voice, excused herself, and went upstairs to her patients. It would be very satisfying to throw something at her aunt, she thought fiercely as she busied herself at the medicine cupboard; it would be wonderful, too, to pack her bags and leave the home for ever and never see Aunt Maria again, only if she did that she would break her promise. Besides, the old people she looked after might miss her; they would certainly suffer from the shortage of staff – Aunt Maria would have difficulty in getting anyone to take her place. Two room buzzers sounded together, both from the first floor, Olympia sighed, hastily finished what she was doing, and went to answer them.

Mrs. Cooper was nothing if not punctual on the following day. Olympia handed over the keys, gave a brief report and rushed away to change. She hadn't expected to get away so early, with luck she would be able to spend most of the afternoon as she had planned after all. She put on the tweed suit she had worn now for a couple of years – a dull, brownish garment of a material which refused to wear out – she would be stuck with it for years, she thought resentfully, tying her head-scarf under her chin and snatching up the leather gloves she had saved so long to buy. Aunt Maria had been disgusted with her for her extravagance in purchasing them; gloves, she had argued, did not need to be of leather, there were several good imitations these days; neither did they have to be purchased at Harrods. British Home Stores, she had continued, warming to her theme, had an enormous variety at a very reasonable price, and it was both unkind and thoughtless of Olympia to waste her aunt's money in such a fashion. That Olympia had worked hard and long for a salary no other girl would have dreamed of accepting seemed to have escaped her mind; when Olympia had reminded her of it, it was to bring down a storm of recrimination on her head. She remembered it now as she let herself out of the door and heaved a sigh of relief at being free once more, even if only for a few hours. She caught the bus going down Primrose Hill, busily planning the hours before her.

Selfridges was crowded. She found her way to the linen department, and uncaring of her aunt's minute instructions about the careful examination of the sheets before she ordered them, chose the first pair she was shown, had them entered on Miss Randle's account, and turned her attention to more interesting merchandise. Coloured sheets, she mused, flowered ones, stripes even, would cheer up the clinical austerity of the rooms at the nursing home at very little extra expense. She had suggested it once and her aunt had been horrified, deploring the regrettably extravagant streak in her niece's character. Olympia wandered along, through the dress department and the coats, feasting her eyes upon the clothes she would like to wear, given the chance, until a glance at the clock caused her to leave the store. It was a pity she had telephoned Sally and cancelled their tea together; she could have fitted it in nicely after all, but she still had several hours to herself. She got on a bus once more, got off at the National Gallery and ran up the steps. On the last step of all she tripped and fell on her face.

The hands which picked her up were large and firm and gentle, they set her on her feet with no fuss, dusted her down, tweaked her head-scarf straight and then dropped lightly on to her shoulders.

Olympia rubbed a sore knee and looked up at her rescuer; a large man, very tall and not so very young; forty, she judged, with pale-coloured hair heavily sprinkled with grey and a handsome face which rather took her breath. Such men seldom came her way, and now, she thought with regret and annoyance, she had to be fool enough to fall down so absurdly – her suit would be a mess too – she glanced down at it and he spoke. He had a nice voice too, slow and deep and faintly accented. 'Not much harm done, I think – sore knees perhaps, and a bruise or two . . .'

She answered him shyly. 'I was really more bothered about my clothes.'

His blue eyes studied her without haste. 'Nothing a clothes brush can't tackle.' He dropped his hands from her shoulders and went on with casual friendliness. 'Were you going to the exhibition? If so, I daresay an attendant could find a brush for you.'

She nodded once more. 'But I think I'd better go home.'

He gave her another long, considered look. 'Surely no need for that? I suggest that you go and tidy yourself, and be sure and wash your grazes with soap and water. I'll wait and we'll walk round together.'

His cool command of the situation should have nettled her, but it didn't. 'But ...' began Olympia.

He interrupted her crisply. 'We will introduce ourselves,' his voice became mild, 'and then all will be most proper, will it not? I'm Waldo van der Graaf,' he held out a large hand and she put hers into it and he wrung it gently.

'Mine's Randle – O-Olympia.'

He showed no signs of amusement but queried: 'You are not married?'

It was more of a statement than a question, and she winced a little that he should have taken it for granted, though heaven knew by the look of her he had no reason to suppose otherwise. She said, 'No,' rather defiantly.

They went inside then and she found herself, after her companion had murmured briefly to one of the attendants, being led away to a cloakroom, where mindful of the large man's words, she washed the dirt from her knees and then stood patiently while the attendant got to work on the stains. She looked a little

16

better then, but still woefully inadequate to be a companion to such a handsome and distinguished-looking man. She went back into the entrance hall, half expecting him to be gone, but he was still standing where she had left him, studying a catalogue in an unconcerned way, as though he had all the time in the world before him. He looked up as she reached him and smiled, and then without speaking took her arm and ushered her into the first room.

They didn't hurry, and she was so absorbed that she didn't notice the time; it was delightful to be with someone who actually listened to her, and even shared her tastes, and when he didn't, refrained from ramming his own down her throat. They were still lingering in the last room when she happened to see a clock.

'I must go,' she declared, appalled. 'It's almost half past four, the bus queues will be packed if I don't hurry – I'll never get back in time.'

He gave her a quick side-glance. 'You have to return at a certain time?'

She told him, guardedly, about Aunt Maria and Mr. Gibson coming to supper. 'So you see, I must . . .' she smiled at him, feeling as though he were an old friend. 'It's been a lovely afternoon, thank you.'

She held out a hand, but intead of shaking it he took it between his own. 'You have to be back by six o'clock? Time enough for a cup of tea together, and it just so happens that I have to go to – er – Hampstead this evening. I should be delighted to offer you a lift in my taxi.'

She eyed him uncertainly. 'But won't it be . . .? That is, you won't mind? And you'll be sure and get me there by six?'

He smiled down at her, kind and reassuring and yet casual. 'Cross my heart – is that not what you say in English?'

They had walked slowly out of the entrance and down the steps as they were talking. 'You're not English?' Olympia wanted to know.

'Dutch, but I come often to England – I have English relations.' He lifted a hand at a passing taxi and settled her into it, then got in beside her. She heard him say: 'Fortnum and Mason, please,' with a sudden childish excitement; she had never been there in her life, not inside at any rate. She said now a little anxiously: 'I'm not dressed for a super place like that,' and was instantly and ridiculously reassured by his quiet: 'You are very nicely dressed, Miss Randle.'

All the same, she was a little apprehensive as they seated themselves in the elegant tea-room; the place seemed to her excited mind to be full of fur coats and what the fashion magazines always referred to as little dresses, which cost the earth, she had no doubt. She took off her headscarf and smoothed her neat head with a nervous hand and met his eyes, twinkling nicely, across the table. 'Tea?' he inquired. 'Earl Grey, I think – and buttered toast and little cakes.' His firm mouth turned its corners up briefly. 'I enjoy your English tea.'

She enjoyed it too; her companion had the gift of making her feel at ease, even amongst the Givenchy scarves and crocodile handbags. She found herself telling him about Aunt Maria and the nursing home and then stopped rather suddenly because she was being disloyal to her aunt and he was, after all, a stranger. He didn't appear to notice her discomfiture, however, but talked on, filling awkward pauses with an easy bland-

18

ness, so that by the time she got up to go she was a little hazy as to what she had actually said.

He talked nothings in the taxi too, so that by the time they arrived outside the nursing home she had quite forgotten, for the time being at least, a good deal of what they had talked about during tea.

He got out with her and walked to the door and when she had bidden him good-bye and opened it, he gave the cold, austere hall the same shrewd look as he had given her, but he made no remark, merely said that he had enjoyed his afternoon without evincing any wish to see her again, as indeed, she had expected. She was not, she reminded herself sadly, the kind of girl men wanted to take out a second time; she had no sparkle, no looks above the ordinary, and living for years with Aunt Maria, who liked to do all the talking, had hardly improved her conversation. She wished him good-bye in a quiet little voice, thanked him again, and went into the house.

If she was more subdued than ever that evening, her aunt was far too absorbed in her conversation with Mr. Gibson to notice; certainly she had no time to question her niece as to how she had spent her afternoon, something for which Olympia was thankful. She got the supper and cleared it away again, then went to her room with the perfectly legitimate excuse that she was on duty early the next morning. But she didn't go to bed immediately; she sat and thought about Mr. van der Graaf; she thought about their tea together and then, a little uneasily, of the things she had told him; she was still hazy as to exactly what she had said, but as she would never see him again, she consoled herself with the fact that it wouldn't really matter, he would have forgotten her already; he had whisked in and out of her life, large and elegant and very sure of himself. Olympia sighed, frowned at her reflection in the old-fashioned dressing-table mirror, and went to bed.

CHAPTER TWO

THE next few days went quietly by. The local doctors made their visits and relations made their infrequent appearance, and Olympia went about her duties with her usual quiet competence, and very much against the counsel of her common sense, found herself thinking far too much about the man she had met so unexpectedly. It took her several days to discipline her thoughts into more workaday channels, and she had just achieved this laudable object when she went to open the street door because the daily maid hadn't come that day, and found him on the doorstep. Not alone – he was with old Doctor Sims. Doctor Sims was an old dear, kind and wise, and despite his advanced years, still clever. He was untidy, too, and rotund and addicted to smoking cigars. He had one in his mouth now; the ash from it fell on to his coat and he flicked it on one side with an impatient finger which scattered it disastrously.

He said cheerfully: 'Morning, Olympia – don't stare so, girl, you've seen me a hundred times, anyone would think that you were seeing a pair of ghosts.' He waved a careless hand at his companion. 'This is Doctor van der Graaf, son of an old friend of mine, now alas, dead. I've brought him along to see Mrs. Parsons.'

Olympia stood aside to allow them to pass her into the hall, said: 'How do you do?' to the Dutchman's sober tie and shut the door carefully behind them. He answered her with a casual friendliness which took away her awkwardness immediately. 'Hullo again –

have the bruises gone?'

She nodded, on the point of finding her surprised tongue, when Doctor Sims asked testily: 'Where's the girl who opens the door? Why are you doing it?'

'She's taken a day off – she does sometimes, and nobody says anything because daily maids are hard to get. My aunt's out. I'll take you up to Mrs. Parsons, shall I?'

The old gentleman grunted, flicked ash on to the pristine floor and took off his overcoat.

'Well run place,' he mumbled to no one in particular. 'Clean – food's quite good too. Warm enough, plenty of bed linen, but it's all too stark, not enough nurses either. Your aunt's a woman to make a success of a place like this though – gets a packet out of it, I don't doubt. But you do the work, don't you, Olympia?'

He started up the stairs with her behind him, trying to think of some suitable reply to make to this remark, and behind her came Doctor van der Graaf, silent but for his few words of greeting. Despite his silence, though, she was intensely aware of him, and as they reached the first floor she was annoyingly sure that her appearance could have been improved upon; her hair had escaped from the severely pinned bun and was bobbing around her ears in wispy curls. She put up a tentative hand and arrested it in mid-air when he said quietly: 'It looks nice like that, leave it alone.'

She didn't turn round, though she put her hand down again as she led the way up the next flight of stairs and then pausing to allow Doctor Sims to regain his breath, started up the last narrow staircase.

Mrs. Parsons shared a room on the top floor with three other old ladies because the pension she received as a rather obscure Civil Servant's widow didn't stretch to anything else. She was very old now, afflicted with a variety of minor ailments and quite alone save for a nephew who came to see her at Christmas, who criticized the treatment she was receiving, presenting her with a box of rather inferior handkerchiefs when he had done so, before returning to some obscure country retreat. No one, certainly not his aunt, took much notice of him, and Olympia, backed up by Doctor Sims, had done her best to act as substitute for the family she no longer had.

She was a garrulous old lady, given to repeating herself continually and forgetting what she had said as soon as she had said it, but the two doctors sat down beside her chair and talked pleasantly about the small things which might amuse her, and listened with patient kindness to her jumbled answers. She had accepted Doctor Sims' companion without surprise, merely stopping to ask him every few minutes what his name might be, and each time he answered with no sign of impatience. Olympia, straightening beds nearby, decided that he was the nicest man she had ever met and certainly the handsomest, and when he looked up suddenly and smiled at her, she smiled back, the whole of her quiet little face lighting up.

The two men went away presently and Olympia stifled disappointment because Doctor van der Graaf said nothing more than a brief good-bye. Making beds after they had gone, she told herself that she had no reason to be disappointed; he had asked after her bruises, hadn't he? and said hullo and good-bye. What more could she expect? Distinguished and good-looking men who wore gold cuff links and silk shirts and exquisitely tailored suits wouldn't be likely to look twice at a rather colourless girl who, even if she had had warning of a meeting, would still have looked unremarkable despite all her best efforts. He had been nice about taking her to tea at Fortnum and Mason, though, and he had told her to leave her hair alone and it had somehow sounded like a compliment.

She dropped the blanket she was spreading and went to the mirror over the washbasin. Her face was faintly flushed with the excitement of the visitors and the exertion of bed-making, so that her hair was still curling in little tendrils round her ears. She gave one an experimental tug and then let it go; the front door below had closed with the decisive snap which was the hallmark of Aunt Maria's comings and goings. Olympia turned away from the mirror, finished the bed and went soberly downstairs; her aunt would expect her to go immediately to her office and render an account of what had happened during her absence.

Aunt Maria dismissed the visitor with a shrug; Doctor Sims had a habit of bringing friends with him from time to time; they seldom returned, she didn't even inquire closely about him, so that Olympia was saved the trouble of saying much about him, something she had felt curiously unwilling to do; he was a secret, a rather nice one and the only one she had. Her aunt dismissed her with a curt nod and sent her back to her duties without any further questions.

Doctor van der Graaf came exactly two days later, although Olympia was unaware of his visit until Miss Snow came fluttering upstairs with a message that she was to go to her aunt's office immediately. Olympia consigned old Mr. Ross, tottering to slow recovery after a stroke, to Miss Snow's care and went slowly downstairs, wondering what she had done wrong now.

She was quite unprepared for the sight of the Dutchman sitting calmly in the chair opposite her aunt's desk, the very picture of a man who was confident that he would get his own way. He got up as she went in, smiling a little at her surprise, and said easily: 'Good afternoon, Miss Randle. I have been persuading your aunt to allow you to act as guide; there are things I wish to purchase and I am woefully ignorant as to how to set about my shopping. I remembered you and I wondered if you would be so kind?'

'Oh, that would . . .' She paused and began again. 'You're very kind to think of me, but I'm working until eight o'clock.'

Miss Randle interrupted her in an irritable manner; she wasn't used to people riding roughshod over her wishes, but she seemed quite unable to argue with this tiresome giant of a man. 'I will make an exception, Olympia, you may take your free time this afternoon, but you will, of course, return to evening duty at half past five.'

It was barely half past two; Olympia murmured dutifully and got herself out of the room; her aunt would have to take over until she got back, there were no other trained nurses on duty – she might change her mind, thought Olympia, desperately tearing off her uniform and putting on the tweed suit like lightning. Thank heaven it was a fine day even if cold. She did her hair with a speed which did nothing to improve her appearance, tucked a silk scarf given her by a grateful patient round her neck, snatched up her gloves and bag and raced upstairs. He was still there. He took a leisurely farewell of her aunt, assured her of his gratitude, opened the door for Olympia and closed it with firmness behind him.

'What do you want to buy?' asked Olympia at once.

He stood on the pavement outside the house, deep in thought. 'Well, let me see, something for Ria – my little daughter, you know. She is almost five years old and very precocious, I'm afraid. Her mother died a week or so after she was born.'

Olympia restrained her feet from the impatient dance she felt like executing; any moment Aunt Maria might change her mind and they were still standing just outside the door. Quite shocked at what he had told her, she said, 'I'm sorry,' and felt inadequate. Of course he would have been married; men like him didn't go through life like monks; perhaps he had loved his wife very much, perhaps he was still grieving for her. She tried again. 'It must be terrible for you.'

He looked taken aback, but only for a moment. 'Ria is a handful,' he said blandly. 'Shall we go?'

They went to Selfridges, this time to the toy department, where, after a prolonged tour of its delights, Olympia, asked to choose a suitable present for a five-year-old girl without worrying too much about the price, picked out a doll's house. It was a thing which she herself would have loved to possess and never had; it was furnished down to the last miniature saucepan in its magnificent kitchen, and was everything which a little girl could wish for. She spent a long time hanging over it, switching on the lights, opening and shutting the miniature doors, rearranging the furniture. When at last she looked up it was to find her companion's blue eyes regarding her with a tolerant patience which coloured her cheeks with guilty pink. She said apologetically: 'I always wanted a doll's house – your little daughter will love this one.'

She watched while he wrote a cheque for it – a fabulous sum, she considered, and fell to wondering how it was that he was able to write cheques when he was a Dutchman, living, presumably, in Holland. She spoke her thought. 'You live in Holland, don't you?'

He smiled. 'Oh, yes – I have a large practice in the country town called Middleburg. That is my home, but I do a good deal of lecturing, some of it in England.'

So that accounted for the cheque book. 'Have you been here ever since we – since you helped me that day?'

'No. I wished to see you again, so I came over three days ago.'

She had nothing to say to that, and anyway the saleslady wanted to talk to him about the packing up of the doll's house. When he turned to her again it was only to say: 'I think we have time for tea before you have to be back. Shall we go to Fortnum and Mason again, or would you prefer somewhere else?'

Olympia could not, from her limited experience, think of any place to better it, so she murmured a polite: 'That would be nice,' while her sober head buzzed with the effort of guessing why he had wanted to see her. They were in the taxi, travelling in a companionable silence, before a possible reason struck her. He was looking for a governess for his small daughter and had picked on her. The possibility of such a miracle filled her with a warm glow of delight, to be instantly quenched by the recollection of her promise to her aunt – only if she were to marry might she leave, Aunt Maria had said. She clenched the cheap handbag on

27

her lap with suddenly desperate fingers so that her companion, watching her from his corner, asked: 'Supposing you tell me what's bothering you?'

Her voice rose several notes in its urgency. 'Nothing – nothing at all.'

He said, his manner very placid, 'We haven't known each other very long, but I hoped you might feel able to confide in me.'

She turned to look at him. 'Confide . . .?' she began, and then: 'In you?'

'Next time, perhaps,' he replied casually as the taxi stopped, and for the rest of their afternoon together, he talked about nothing in particular. Only as he walked up to the front door of the nursing home with her and she put out her hand did he say, 'I'm coming in – I wish to see your aunt.'

Olympia allowed her hand to drop back to her side, pausing before she opened the door. 'Why?' she asked.

'I should like her to understand quite clearly that I wish to get to know you,' he said to astonish her.

She stared up at him for a long moment and spoke wistfully: 'It won't be any good, you know, she won't let me go . . .' And she was unaware of what she had said.

He smiled, but his voice was firm. 'I think that she will.'

Olympia opened the door. She had never known anyone get the better of Aunt Maria, but presumably there had to be a first time for everything. She wished him success from the bottom of her heart. 'I'll see if she's in her office,' she offered, and left him standing in the chill of the hall.

She was back within a minute. 'Aunt will be pleased

to see you,' she told him, and shivered. He paused beside her and put a hand on her shoulder. 'This damned cold hall,' he remarked feelingly, then astonished her by asking, 'Why are you called Olympia?'

She smiled then and her eyes widened and twinkled at him so that she looked pretty. 'Father was an archaeologist, he met Mother during a dig in Greece. I – I like it.'

'So do I.' He went through the door behind her as he spoke, leaving her to run downstairs and change back into uniform.

She had no moment of time in which to think about him after that; her aunt had done none of the things the nurses did towards easing the evening's work. There were beds to turn down, medicines to give, supper trays to lay, the old people to help with their preparations for bed, and Miss Snow, if she were to be believed, had been left to cope with the patients' teas all by herself and was so incensed in consequence that Olympia took ten minutes of her precious time to soothe her down and persuade her not to give in her notice then and there. Perhaps, she thought, as she dished out the light supper at a great rate, it would be as well if Aunt Maria told Doctor van der Graaf not to call again.

But she hadn't, or if she had, he had taken no notice of her, for he came again the very next day, this time in the morning just as Olympia was going off duty for the split her aunt insisted was necessary for her to take twice a week – that meant that she went on duty at half past seven in the morning, was free from half past ten until one o'clock, and then worked through the remainder of the day until the night staff came on, a wretched arrangement which no hospital nurse would have tolerated unless circumstances made it vital. She found him standing in the hall on the way down to her room and had given him a rather surprised good morning, followed by an inquiry as to whether he wished to see her aunt again.

'God forbid,' he said quietly. 'I've come for you. Your aunt gave me the times of your off duty – I thought we might go somewhere and have coffee – lunch is out of the question, I take it.'

He stood looking at her, his head on one side. 'I thought that the modern nurse had improved her lot to a certain extent; it seems that doesn't apply to this place.'

'My aunt hasn't many nurses – only me and Mrs. Cooper, and she's part-time. Miss Snow and Mrs. Drew aren't trained – they're very good, though.'

'You do not complain. I suspect that the writer of that poem – I can't remember much of it – had you in mind when she wrote: "While just the art of being kind is all the sad world needs." '

She was quite shocked. 'Oh, you mustn't think that; I'm not kind at all. Sometimes I could leave everything just as it is, and run through the door – if you knew how I want to escape . . .'

'But you don't?'

'I promised . . . I explained to you . . .'

He didn't answer, only smiled at her and told her to go and put on something warm; the March wind was cold, as though it were making a last effort to keep April at bay. Olympia put on the suit again and tied a scarf over her hair because the only hat she had was a dreary affair reserved for church. They were going to have coffee, he had said – there were plenty of small cafés not too far away, and none of them had a smart clientele. She sighed unconsciously as she ran upstairs to join him; perhaps today, if he had got his way with Aunt Maria, he would offer her a job. Her heart leapt at the prospect and she beamed at him as she reached the hall.

There was a taxi waiting and she looked at him questioningly as she got in. 'A wretched day,' he offered. 'I thought we might go somewhere warm and cheerful.'

They went to a small Viennese café near Bond Street and over their delicious coffee and creamy cakes, Olympia found herself talking to her companion as though she had known him all her life. Indeed, afterwards, when she was back in the home, once more at work, she chided herself for talking too much. She would have to guard her tongue, for he had a way of asking questions ... she frowned, not that that mattered; he had said nothing about seeing her again.

But it was the first of a succession of similar outings. Olympia, longing to ask him what he had said to her aunt so that lady had raised no objections to his continued visits, made wild, unsatisfying guesses as to his reasons for wishing to seek her company; surely if he had wanted her for a job he would have mentioned it by now. But his visits continued, sometimes with Doctor Ross, but more often his arrival was timed to coincide with her off-duty. It was at the end of a second week of afternoon walks and leisurely coffee drinking that she ventured to ask him if he was on holiday. They were strolling round the Zoo at the time, taking advantage of the thin April sunshine and watching the antics of the monkeys.

He turned to look at her. 'No,' he told her with deliberation, 'I have been attending a seminar – it finishes tomorrow. I am also visiting an aunt – an Englishwoman, the widow of my father's elder brother.' He smiled suddenly. 'I should like you to meet her. You are free tomorrow afternoon, are you not?'

She nodded.

'Good – I will call for you about two o'clock.'

'Then you will be going back to Middleburg?'

'Yes.' They strolled on in silence while she thought that this was the end – well, almost the end, of their friendship. She was going to miss him very much, there was no denying that fact; what to him had been a small interlude had been for her a delightful few weeks in her dull life. Of course, she knew very little about him and nothing at all of his life – just as well perhaps, since she was unlikely to have a place in it after tomorrow. These rather unhappy thoughts were interrupted by his cheerful: 'How about tea? There's time enough before you have to go back.'

She dressed with extra care the following afternoon; the same tweed suit, of course, but having received her miserable salary a day or so earlier, she had bought a new woolly from Marks and Spencer – a pale apricot which gave her face a pleasant glow and cheered up the suit enormously; she had bought a brown velvet bow to set in front of her bun of hair, too; studying herself in the long looking glass at the back of the hall, she decided that she was at least presentable although woefully dowdy. It was to be hoped that the aunt wasn't a fashionable old lady who would despise her.

It seemed at first that her forebodings might prove true. They had walked, she and the doctor, for it was a fine day and his aunt lived in Little Venice, in one of the terraces facing the Grand Union Canal. They had entered the park through the Gloucester Gate and crossed it diagonally to arrive within a stone's throw of a row of substantial houses.

'A flat?' hazarded Olympia, gazing up at their solid fronts, with their well-painted doors and window boxes. Her companion took her arm and guided her through a solid gate set between equally solid walls.

'No – the whole house.' He pealed the bell and the door was opened with alacrity by a neat elderly woman who smiled at them as they went in. In the hall he helped Olympia out of her jacket, divested himself of his own coat and threw it on a chair in what she considered to be a rather careless manner, and upon the elderly woman begging them to go upstairs, did so, taking Olympia with him.

The room they entered was very fine; large, and filled with large furniture too, covered with silver photo frames enclosing a variety of out-of-date photographs, an astonishing assortment of china and silver and the whole shrouded with heavy dark blue curtains half drawn over the old-fashioned Nottingham lace which screened the windows. And the lady who came across the room to meet them matched it very nicely for size; she was tall and stout, with a straight back and a proudly held head crowned with iron-grey hair, dressed smoothly. She might have been any age from the lightness of her step and the elegant timelessness of her clothes. Olympia's heart sank; she had no idea why Doctor van der Graaf had brought her here with him, but she felt sure that it had been a mistake. Only his firm hand under her arm, propelling her gently forward, prevented her from turning tail and racing away from someone she felt instinctively would make her feel dowdier than she already was.

She couldn't have been more mistaken; her companion's, 'Hullo, Aunt Betsy,' changed everything. The majestic, elegant woman surging towards her wasn't anyone to be nervous of after all; her exquisitely made up face wore a beaming smile and her voice when she spoke could only be described as cosy.

'Waldo, dear boy – and this is Olympia.' She turned her beam upon her. 'Dear child, how accurately he described you to me. Come and sit down and tell me all about yourself.'

Olympia sat, not sure if her hostess really wanted the details of her rather prosaic life, but she was saved from answering because Aunt Betsy went on almost without pause: 'That is a charming colour – one of Marks and Spencer's, of course. You should wear it often – I always buy my woollies there.'

This reassuringly homely remark got them well launched into a comfortable chat about clothes, with her hostess sustaining a monologue which needed nothing added save a nod and a smile from time to time, which gave Olympia the opportunity to think that she liked Mrs. van der Graaf very much and how nice it would have been if Aunt Maria had been like her.

'Pink, with marabou round the hem,' said her hostess, cutting into her thoughts, and followed that with: 'Yes, yes, Waldo, you are a patient man, I know, but I can see that you wish to be alone with Olympia. I shall go and see if Mary has the tea ready, but in half an hour I shall return, I warn you – I like my tea at four o'clock and it is now precisely half past three.' She sailed majestically to the door, smiling at them in turn and stopped to peck the doctor's cheek when he opened the door for her.

Olympia, sitting on the edge of a large brocade-

34

covered chair, watched her departure with some surprise. When the doctor had shut the door behind his aunt, she asked: 'Whatever did she mean? Why do you want to be alone ...' She stopped; of course it was about the job he was going to offer her – he had brought her along to be vetted by his aunt before offering it to her and presumably she was satisfactory. She sighed with relief. 'Oh, so you are going to offer me the job after all.'

He looked astonished, but only for a moment; the astonishment was replaced by amusement. 'With my little daughter in mind?'

'Well, of course.' Olympia hesitated. 'You did say that she was badly in need of someone to mother her.' She went a little pink. 'I'm sorry, I shouldn't have said anything – it was only a guess because that's why I thought you wanted to get to know me, and anyway, even if ...' she looked down at her clenched hands in her lap. 'Aunt Maria wouldn't allow it.'

He strolled across the room and sat down facing her. 'I asked you to come here with me because I wanted to talk to you and I dislike holding private conversations in taxis or some tea-shop or other, not because I wanted Aunt Betsy to look you over.' He smiled nicely at her. 'She knows that I am quite capable of doing my own looking over. And you made no mistake, it does concern you and Ria, but not, I think, in quite the manner you have assumed. I have no intention of offering you a job, Olympia. I should like you to marry me.'

She had the peculiar sensation that she wasn't sitting on the enormous chair at all, but floating in nothing. The room came and went in a rather alarming manner and the silence which followed his words seemed to go on for ever. Presently she found her voice to say: 'You

35

did say marry you?'

'Yes.' He was sitting back, quite at ease.

There were a great many things she could have said, but she discarded them all in favour of a bald: 'Why?'

'Because it is obviously such a suitable arrangement for both of us . . .'

She didn't let him finish. 'You can't really mean that!' and knew as she said it that he most certainly did.

He continued just as though she had said nothing at all. 'You see, Olympia, I need someone to care for Ria, to love her, if possible, and check her tantrums and, as you so aptly put it, mother her. I need someone to run my house too – I have an admirable housekeeper, but she cannot play hostess to my friends or arrange dinner parties or make a home of it. And you – you want to get away from that domineering . . . I beg your pardon – from your aunt and that dreary home. You told me yourself that you had promised to remain there unless someone asked you to marry him. Well, I am that someone; we shall both be helping each other, and I think we have seen sufficient of each other now to know that we shall get along very well. You won't see a great deal of me, but being a nurse, you are already aware of the kind of life I lead, and we neither of us complicate the situation by our emotions.'

Olympia received this dry-as-dust speech in silence and took her time in answering it. 'I don't quite understand why you haven't just asked me to be a governess – I mean you don't really want a wife, do you?'

He considered gravely before he replied. 'A wife in the accepted sense, no. But as I told you, I need someone to run my home and act as hostess and of course, care for Ria, someone who is a good friend, who will fit into my way of living.' His smile was kind; he was quite unaware of her poor trampled feelings. 'Besides, I enjoy your company, Olympia. You are restful and sensible and even-tempered.'

She felt almost insulted; there were surely other adjectives he might have used. Who wanted to be any of these worthy things? And he was wrong about her even temper; she was aware that beneath her serene front she was nicely on the boil.

'You might come to dislike me in a month or so – even after a number of years.'

He shook his head and declared positively: 'No, my opinions do not change easily. I like you, Olympia, and shall always do so, whatever happens.'

He had an answer for everything and she knew nothing at all about him, only the few bare facts he had told her, and yet she trusted him, and he had said that he would like her for his wife – an unusual kind of wife, she thought ruefully, but half a loaf was better than no bread. She was unhappy in the house on Primrose Hill and as far as she could see into the future, she had no hope of leaving it unless she married. Aunt Maria was barely middle-aged and likely to live for many years to come. She had an unhappy little picture of herself in ten, twenty years' time, with not even youth to give her ordinary face an edge of attractiveness. Undoubtedly this was her chance – she frowned as she remembered the old people she looked after. 'There's no one to do my work if I go,' she told him in a small voice. 'Mrs. Cooper's only part-time, there has to be a trained nurse ... besides, there will be no one at night to get up ...'

The doctor's eyes narrowed. 'You get up at night as well as working during the day?'

'Well, I have to.' She spoke almost defensively. 'If something happens that needs a trained nurse.'

'So that is why you have shadows under your eyes – you are also too thin.'

She brushed this aside almost impatiently; what did it matter if she was thin and plain with it? He wasn't marrying her for her looks, was he? She spoke suddenly. 'It's not because you pity me, is it?'

His lips twitched a little at the fierceness of her look. 'No, I don't pity you, Olympia.' He had got up and was standing by one of the windows, looking at her. 'I think you mustn't hunt around in your head for reasons which aren't reasons at all. I have told you why I should like to marry you; there are no other reasons – none at all. But I have taken you by surprise, haven't I? Perhaps you would like a little time to decide?'

'Yes, please.'

'I'll call and see you tomorrow. You are off duty in the morning, aren't you?' He added kindly: 'And if it will help you in any way, I will undertake to find a nurse to replace you, immediately.'

'Oh, will you really? I . . .' She stopped because the door had been thrown open and Mrs. van der Graaf, followed by Mary carrying the tea-tray, came in.

She began to talk the moment she was in the room, but not about them; every other subject under the sun, Olympia couldn't fail to notice, but not one question, not even a look of inquiry. They ate their tea, borne along on a tide of cheerful conversation which Olympia found soothing after her rather surprising talk with the doctor. And when she went back with him presently, by taxi this time, the subject lying so heavily on her mind wasn't mentioned. Indeed, back in her little basement room, she wondered if she had dreamed the whole thing. An observation of her aunt's came into her head. 'Sleep on it,' she would say. Olympia slept on it.

CHAPTER THREE

SHE slept soundly, with no half-hoped-for dreams to offer her their guidance, and the pleased old faces which welcomed her as she began her morning's work offered her a mute but sound reason for refusing the doctor's offer, although he had said – no, promised – that he would find someone to take her place. But her mind was made up for her in quite another manner; she had been getting the old people on the top floor out of their beds when her aunt had walked in. She had nodded briefly to the patients, for this wasn't her usual mid-morning round when she stopped and spoke briefly to each one of them, careful never to give them a chance to say much themselves, but now her interest was centred upon her niece.

'Come outside, Nurse Randle,' she invited in a voice which boded no good for Olympia, and once they were outside on the little landing, 'I have been considering the matter, Olympia, and I have decided that there is no point in seeing any more of Doctor van der Graaf.' She frowned. 'Indeed, I cannot imagine how I ever allowed myself to be persuaded in the first place – however, I feel sure that by now he will be only to glad to have a decision made for him. I feel sure too that he must be heartily sick of you by now; probably he is too kind a man to say so. When he comes again I shall tell him that you have decided not to see him again.'

Olympia choked back rage, humiliation and sheer fright that what her aunt had said might be true – but how could it be? She said in a quiet little voice which gave no hint of her strong feelings, 'You are mistaken, Aunt, and I can't see why I shouldn't go out with Doctor van der Graaf if I want to. He's coming to see me this morning . . .'

'He's here,' interposed the doctor from the stairs behind them, and before either of the ladies could say a word: 'Good morning, and before you say anything further, Miss Randle, I have asked Olympia to be my wife . . .' He paused for a second and shot a glance at her and something in her white face must have given him his answer, for he went on smoothly: 'And she has consented.' He crossed the landing and took Olympia's hand in his and smiled down at her, and she, feeling that events were moving of their own accord without any help from her, smiled nervously back.

'I shall not allow . . .' began Miss Randle, much incensed.

'Oh, but I think you will. Has not Olympia honoured her promise to you for a number of years? Now it is your turn to do the same, Miss Randle.' His voice was bland enough, but he didn't smile and his eyes were cool.

'I . . .' began Olympia, wishing to put her oar in, and was hushed before she could say another word by the doctor who went on in a conversational manner, 'A quiet wedding, I think, if Olympia agrees. We neither of us have many friends in London, and no family. You will, of course, have no objection to her leaving at once, Miss Randle? I have been fortunate enough to find someone who will take her place immediately.'

'Now?' They spoke together, staring at him, Miss Randle with a furious face suffused with wrath, Olympia with delight and relief and a kind of wonder.

Any minute now, she thought, I shall open my eyes and find I've been dreaming.

'Now,' said Doctor van der Graaf in a gentle voice which nevertheless invited obedience, 'if you will pack what you need, dear girl, I will wait for you.'

Aunt Maria looked to be on the point of apoplexy. 'There is no one to do her work – I cannot possibly manage – this is most unethical!'

He agreed cheerfully and went on smoothly: 'The nurse I have secured will arrive this afternoon, Miss Randle. She will, of course, expect to be paid the salary agreed by the General Nursing Council, and since you have mentioned the word unethical, I wonder what salary you have been paying Olympia? Not, I fancy, the amount to which she has been entitled.' He gave her a bland smile and pushed Olympia gently towards the stairs. 'Go along,' he told her, 'though perhaps you had better say good-bye to your patients first.'

She looked at him; it was like a dream still. 'I feel very mean leaving them.'

'You shall come back and visit them, that's a promise. Besides, they will be delighted to know that you are going to be married. Everyone likes a wedding, you know.'

It took her half an hour to pack her things, and barely five minutes in which to say good-bye to Aunt Maria, who washed her hands of her in no uncertain terms, predicted that no good would come of it and that Olympia would live to rue the day. 'And don't come running back to me, my girl, for I'll not lift a finger to help you, just you remember that.'

'I'm sorry you're angry,' said Olympia, anxious to part friends even though she was glad to be going.

'Angry?' her aunt snapped back. 'Of course I'm

angry; the years I've devoted to you, given you a home, educated and clothed you . . .'

'And the years I've worked for you for little more than pocket money!' retaliated Olympia, stung to sudden indigantion. 'And I would have gone on for the rest of my life if Doctor van der Graaf hadn't come along.'

'And may you never live to regret the day,' was her aunt's parting shot.

There was obviously no more to be said; Olympia, with a murmured good-bye, left her sitting at her desk, her head already bowed over the papers before her.

Doctor van der Graaf was waiting in the hall, pacing up and down, his hands behind his back, deep in thought. He shot her a penetrating look as she went towards him and said on a half laugh: 'Don't stop to have second thoughts. I know exactly what is in your mind; regrets and a half-formed resolution to make a martyr of yourself – and how will your aunt manage and what about the old people.' He caught her hand in his. 'Olympia, I promise you that everything will be all right. Will you trust me?'

She studied his kind blue eyes. 'Yes.' She even achieved some sort of a smile, because no man wanted a watering pot for a wife. 'Where am I to go?'

'Aunt Betsy, just until I can make arrangements for us to get married.'

'Oh, I couldn't!' They were getting into the taxi which the doctor had prudently kept waiting. He said placidly as he got in beside her:

'Do you dislike her so much? I admit she's form-idable in appearance, but she has the kindest heart imaginable – besides, she likes you.'

She answered him a little breathlessly; things had

happened so fast that she felt at that moment that she would never catch up with them. 'Does she? I like her too, only I thought . . .'

He observed unexpectedly: 'You have never had a chance to spread your wings, have you, Olympia? I think that you will find the world full of people who will like you.'

'Aunt Maria always told me . . .' began Olympia a little unhappily.

'Your Aunt Maria,' said the doctor deliberately, 'is an odious woman, bent on making you her slave for as long as she needed you and taking gross advantage of your gentle nature. She is making a fortune from that nursing home of hers, and although I grant you that it is well run and the patients cared for adequately, she does it purely for business reasons and not out of pity for her less fortunate fellow beings. She is a hard woman and you are well shot of her.'

Olympia was regarding him with an awakened interest; he had never talked like this before, he seemed suddenly a great deal younger and much more approachable.

'But she told me that she was only just able to make ends meet – that's why she didn't pay me very much.'

'How much?'

She mentioned the miserable sum and was answered by an indignant: 'Good lord, barely enough to keep you in stockings – or is it tights?' His eye surveyed the tweed suit. 'So that's why you wear that thing all the time.'

She sat up very straight, her voice tart. 'That is very rude,' she told him. 'It is – was – quite a good tweed when I bought it.'

44

He grinned, quite unabashed. 'I'm sorry. Does it help if I tell you that you would look nice in anything? And dear girl, since we are to be man and wife, let us be honest with each other. We are already good friends, let us remain so, with no false pride between us, and if we must, let us argue and quarrel and make it up again, just because we are friends, and more than anything else, let us enjoy each other's company.'

Olympia received this speech with mixed feelings; the doctor sounded so very sure of himself, rather like a cook, who, having got hold of a good recipe, was convinced that come what may, it would turn out to be a success. She nodded, bolstered up by a determination to make their marriage succeed.

She was given a welcome such as she had never had before in her life. Mrs. van der Graaf, it seemed, could think of nothing nicer than that Olympia should stay with her for as long as she wished. She was swept upstairs, her hostess steaming ahead of the convoy, as it were, with Olympia, flanked by Mary, and the doctor, burdened with her luggage, bringing up the rear. The stairs led to a landing with four doors. Mrs. van der Graaf opened one of them and ushered her party inside. The room was not over-large, but by Olympia's standards, the epitome of luxury. The furniture was painted white and the bed was covered with a pink satin bedspread and eiderdown which looked far too magnificent for use.

There were a great many little table lamps dotted about, with frilly shades tied with velvet ribbons, and they and the curtains and carpet were of a deeper shade of pink with a delicate pattern of blue upon them. It was the sort of bedroom any girl would have loved; perhaps a little exaggerated in its prettiness, but to Olympia, fresh from her austere little room, it was perfection. She stood speechless while Mary disposed of her luggage and Mrs. van der Graaf inspected the small pile of books on the bedside table, giving it her opinion that a few magazines wouldn't come amiss. She then tweaked the counterpane into even smoother folds, begged Olympia to remove her coat and tidy herself and then come downstairs for a nice glass of sherry before lunch.

They drank it in the sitting-room and the conversation was quite impersonal, sustained almost wholly by the doctor and his aunt. Presently, however, what with the sherry and the return of her self-confidence Olympia began to join in the talk, and because both aunt and nephew shared the gift of putting people at their ease, she began to feel normal again, and not someone living in a dream, although heaven knew that life seemed strange enough at the moment. They were on the point of going in to lunch when her hostess remarked, 'You must be wondering why I haven't wished you happiness, Olympia, but you looked ... never mind that now. But I do, child, wholeheartedly. You will both of you be very happy.'

She nodded her head in deep satisfaction and led the way to the dining-room.

The doctor left after lunch and as she had had no chance to speak to him alone, Olympia saw him preparing to leave with something like panic. He wished her good-bye matter-of-factly and added, '*Tot ziens*,' and when she wanted to know what that had meant, said: 'I suppose "Until we meet again" is as good a translation as any.'

'When shall I see you?' she wanted to know in a

46

voice which held sudden panic.

'This evening. I thought that we might go out and celebrate, you and I. Would you like that?'

She nodded, enchanted at the idea, then remembered unhappily: 'I haven't anything to wear – I couldn't possibly go, I haven't even got a party dress.'

He was at the door, looking very large in his coat and very reassuring too. 'My dear, my aunt will take you out with her this afternoon and you shall choose everything you need – my wedding present to you.'

She thanked him shyly and he bent and kissed her cheek, rather awkwardly, as though he wasn't sure about it.

The afternoon was the most wonderful she had ever known; it was as if all the birthday treats, Christmas parties and presents which she had never had, combined together to make her wildest dreams come true. They went to Harrods, driven there in an elderly Rolls-Royce by an equally elderly chauffeur, and once in the store they repaired to the Gown department where Mrs. van der Graaf, apparently a well-known customer, commanded instant attention. Seated bolt upright and with the head saleswoman in close attendance, she began briskly: 'Now, Olympia, look around you and choose a few dresses to try on.' She peered into a little notebook she had taken from her handbag. 'Let me see – a couple of evening dresses, I think, and something pretty for dinner – a suit and a light coat and something for the day – undies, of course – but let us get the dresses first.'

Olympia heard her out, her eyes getting rounder and rounder. She fastened them upon the saleswoman who retreated to a tactful distance while Olympia said in a frenzied whisper. 'Mrs. van der Graaf, I couldn't possibly – I think there's some mistake. Why, that's several outfits, not just one, and this ...' she looked around her at the opulence of their surroundings, 'isn't the right department – it's the model gowns, far too expensive.'

Mrs. van der Graaf smiled with kindly amusement. 'Dear child, I suppose Waldo neglected to tell you that he was a rich man? I thought so. I assure you that you can choose anything you like without fear of bankrupting him.'

Olympia had caught sight of a blue confection draped tantalizingly over an elegant chair. 'Oh,' she breathed, 'I didn't know. Will you tell me if I spend too much money?'

Her companion reassured her on this point and suggested that she might like to take a closer look at the blue dress, something which she was only too pleased to agree to.

The ball had been set rolling; the dress was pronounced to be exactly right, an exquisite fit and just the thing for her. So for that matter was the deceptively simple cream organza the saleswoman offered, also the deep pink chiffon, with its long full sleeves and demure high neck, so right for a quiet little dinner party. Feeling that she would wake at any moment and find herself back in the unwelcoming chilly hall of the nursing home, Olympia chose a jersey dress in chocolate brown, and because it had been so hard to fix her choice, added a leaf green one to it. A tweed suit came next, all honey browns and purples and greens, and a camel coat to go over the dresses, because, as Mrs. van der Graaf pointed out, it was still only early spring and chilly. She topped this collection with a trouser suit which had taken her fancy, and then, engulfed in sudden horrified realization of the cost of them all, appealed to her hostess. 'I can't, you know,' she declared earnestly, 'I simply can't – this lot must have cost a bomb!'

Mrs. van der Graaf blinked. 'I told you that I would warn you if you got too extravagant, Olympia,' and added in a businesslike manner, 'Shoes – and a pair of those boots girls wear nowadays.'

Olympia submitted meekly but with pleasure. Boots were chosen, the kind of footwear she had never been allowed to have, or indeed could have afforded – shoes were chosen too, evening slippers and walking shoes, elegant trifles which she would, presumably, wear as a matter of course during the day and every day. Olympia, looking, if only she had known it, like a little girl seeing a Christmas tree for the first time, a kind of miracle. But they hadn't finished with her yet; she was borne away to the undies department where, surrounded by silk and chiffon and nylon of every colour of the rainbow, she chose the lovely things she had so often gazed at in shop windows and never thought to have. Watching these expensive trifles being tenderly packed between layers of tissue paper, she found herself wondering what Aunt Maria would say if she could see her now.

They returned in time for tea, a meal which Mrs. van der Graaf was loath to miss but which Olympia would cheerfully have gone without so that she might have followed Bates the chauffeur and Mary up the stairs to her room with all those heavenly boxes and packages. But tea was pleasant, nonetheless, with her hostess giving her little thumbnail sketches of her nephew; they were vague, though, and prevented her from asking the direct questions she was dying to ask; supposedly she would have to ask them of Waldo.

She was dressed and ready far too soon, despite the delays occasioned by the trying on of the various garments hung carefully in the vast wardrobe in her room, so it was with a good half hour to spare that she went down to the sitting-room, to fidget around until the doctor made his appearance. But the wait had been worth while; he stopped in his tracks as he encountered her anxious gaze, his brows raised in a surprise which for her was the best of compliments, especially when it came from a man as good-looking and well dressed as he.

His voice dropped pleasantly into the little silence. 'Delightful, Olympia – you take my breath.'

She said ingenuously: 'Oh, do I?' and smiled widely at him. 'I'm so glad; I wanted to look as nice as possible because you've given me such a mass of gorgeous clothes. I want to thank you.'

He had come to stand beside her and was smiling down at her with gentle amusement. 'I see that I have thanks enough – you look like the princess in the fairy story.'

'You mean the ugly duckling who turned into a swan,' she corrected him.

'No,' he shook his head, 'a princess. Where is my aunt?'

'She went to her room to fetch something.'

'A woman of tact. I have something for you, Olympia.'

A ring; sapphires and diamonds in a curious setting, and even she, who was ignorant of such things, knew that it was valuable. As he put it on her finger the unwelcome thought that it might have belonged to his first wife crossed her mind and she stiffened.

He read her thought. 'No, it was never in the possession of Estelle,' he told her. 'It is very old and has been in my family for many years. It was my mother's.'

She had flushed a little because he had seen so easily what she had been thinking, but she looked at him frankly now and said in a shy voice: 'Thank you very much, I'll treasure it, and I'm sorry I thought that – I should have known better.'

His brows lifted. 'Why should you? You know very little about me, after all.' He greeted his aunt as she came in, leaving her with a feeling that she had been snubbed, but she shook the feeling off; it would never do if she were to be sensitive about everything he said; they were friends, were they not? He should feel free to say anything he liked to her and she must learn to receive it in like vein, so she turned a tranquil, smiling face to him when he asked her if she was ready, and stood quietly while Mrs. van der Graaf examined her ring, talked about it for a few minutes, and then bade her get her coat. Olympia made for the door, then paused. In the excitement of shopping that afternoon there was one thing which they had forgotten; she had no coat. Nothing – no power on earth would make her wear the camel coat over the delicious blue dress she was wearing. She was on the point of saying that she didn't need a coat anyway, even though she would risk getting her death of cold, when the doctor murmured: 'Ah, yes – I had quite forgotten,' and caught her by the arm and marched her into the hall, where draped over a chair was exactly the coat she would have chosen had she been buying one for herself. A rich dark brown velvet, severely cut, with a long wide skirt to it and a little upstanding collar. Exactly right. She drew in her breath like an excited child and gave him a look of delight. 'Oh, Waldo – it's super,' and then in faint reproach, 'You couldn't have forgotten about it . . .'

He grinned. 'You like it? Good.' He held it for her to put on and she turned and twisted before the big gilded mirror, preening herself. 'Thank you, Waldo, thank you a thousand times. I've never had so many beautiful things before – it's wonderful, almost too wonderful to last.'

He made no reply to this childish remark, but ushered her out into the street to the waiting taxi and during the short journey talked placidly about nothing in particular.

They dined at the Coq d'Or, pink and plush and exactly right as a background for the blue dress. Olympia, smitten into dumbness, allowed herself to be seated at a table which she realized was excellently placed, both for seeing and being seen, and she was a little surprised at the number of people who greeted her companion; he was well known, it seemed. She was shy of these strangers, but she had natural good manners and received their good wishes and congratulations with composure even while she hoped that they might be left in peace; there was so much she wanted to know from her future husband, but somehow there never seemed an opportunity to talk to him for more than a few minutes at a time. She ate her way through the superb meal, answering her companion's remarks rather at random, and wondering if the dreamy feeling which she was experiencing was the result of delayed shock at the sudden change of her fortunes, or a little too much of the champagne they were drinking. It wasn't until they were sitting over their coffee that she said suddenly, encouraged by his quiet friendliness and the Dutch courage acquired by the wine, 'I don't know anything at all about Ria, or you.'

He regarded her with a thoughtful frown and took so long to answer that she began to think that she had annoyed him in some way, but when at length he spoke his voice was just as placid as usual. 'I believe that the nicest way to get to know both of us will be to live with us – don't you agree?' He didn't give her a chance to answer, but went on smoothly: 'Would you like to go on somewhere and dance, or shall we sit here and discuss our wedding plans?'

Her ear caught the faint reluctance in his voice when he had mentioned dancing. 'I'd like to talk,' she told him, and was pleased to see that he had wanted to talk too.

'Would you agree to two weeks' time? ten days, if I can arrange things by then – I take it that you would like a quiet wedding?' and when she nodded: 'Get what you need in the way of clothes – something you won't need to change if possible; I shall be able to spare only a short time and we shall have to return to Middelburg after the ceremony. Shall you mind?'

She wondered, fleetingly, what he would have done if she had said that she did mind. 'Not at all,' she replied politely, 'there isn't anyone . . .' she broke off and went on a little awkwardly: 'I don't suppose Aunt Maria will want to come.'

He smiled a little. 'How about Doctor Sims giving you away? I believe he would love to, and is there anyone else you would like to ask?'

'Mrs. Cooper, she works for my aunt – she's always been so sweet to me.'

They talked for a little longer before they finally

returned to the darkened house; Mrs. van der Graaf had retired to bed and there was no sign of Mary. The doctor let them in with his key and once inside showed no sign of wishing to leave but ushered Olympia into the small sitting-room leading from the dining-room, where he invited her to sit down.

'Stay there,' he urged her. 'There'll be coffee in the kitchen.'

He was back five minutes later with a tray which he put on the table beside her, before stretching himself out comfortably in the armchair opposite hers.

'Thank you for my super evening,' said Olympia, pouring coffee.

'The first of many, I hope, although I should point out that I am, for the most part, occupied with the practice. Will you enjoy being a doctor's wife?'

She had a vision of herself running his house – very efficiently, of course – looking after Ria, giving a hand with the patients, and of course being an intelligent listener when he wanted to talk. Perhaps marriage to him wasn't going to be quite what she had dreamed of, but at least she would have a happy, busy life doing all the things housewives did. She had quite, for the moment, forgotten that he was a rich man and might have a different way of life from the one she envisaged.

They sat for quite some time, talking comfortably about nothing in particular and it was only when Waldo got up to go that he mentioned that he would be going back to Holland early the next day. 'I shan't see you for a time, I'm afraid,' he told her in the easy tones of an old friend, 'but I shall try and get over before the wedding, even if only for a day.'

Olympia thought this a piece of extravagance, but she said nothing as she walked with him to the door so that she might bolt it after him. On its threshold he kissed her, a light kiss on her cheek and perhaps not very satisfactory. She went up to bed reflecting that he needed to get used to the idea of marrying again; no doubt he found endearments of any sort still painful after the death of his wife. A romantic girl still, she felt sure that he must have loved Estelle dearly. She undressed slowly, savouring the new dress and the delicate underwear, telling herself firmly that she was a lucky girl, although the face which looked back at her from the mirror wore an expression of unconscious wistfulness.

But it was impossible to remain wistful for long. Waldo might not be there, but as his aunt pointed out, that was a good thing, for there was a great deal to do. Olympia was whisked off to a hairdresser to have her silky abundance of hair trimmed and dressed with an expertise which turned her ordinary little face into something almost pretty. There was the wedding outfit too; bearing in mind the remarks Waldo had made about losing no time after the ceremony, Olympia had discarded for good the vague dreams she had nourished about white satin and gauze; probably he had no idea that a girl set great store upon such things, and if she had mentioned it would have changed his plans in order to accommodate her, however inconvenient to himself; something she could not allow.

As it was, she could not help but be satisfied with the dress and jacket she finally decided upon. It was of fine wool in a rich honey colour, very plainly cut and horribly expensive, and because after all it was her wedding, she bought a hat, an extravagant affair, small and head-hugging with honey-coloured roses bunched at the back. There were shoes and gloves and handbag too, and trying them on a little anxiously before the mirror in the pretty bedroom, she hoped that it was the kind of outfit of which the doctor would approve. The hat was rather a giveaway, but she could take it off after the ceremony if he wanted her to, for she hardly expected him to like the idea of looking like a honeymoon couple. There was to be no honeymoon, anyway; she was to be plunged straight into her future life and perhaps, all things considered, that would be a good thing too.

She didn't see him until the evening before the wedding was to take place and then only for a very short time; just long enough to meet the best man, an English cousin of sorts, the doctor explained, Bill Bentinck by name, big and thick-set and obviously an old and good friend. Olympia liked him even though they exchanged a bare dozen words.

The church was deeply quiet and almost empty when Olympia arrived there with Doctor Sims. She paused on its steps to brush down her companion, for as usual he had been careless with his cigar ash, and when they went inside, the aisle, even in such a very small church as this one, seemed a great length so that she had time to change her mind at least twice about marrying the doctor before she reached his side, but her last-minute doubts vanished when she caught his eye and found him smiling at her in an understanding way. She fetched a sigh of relief then, because there was no more time in which to have doubts, and took the hand he held out to her.

There seemed barely time to cut the cake and drink the champagne which Mrs. van der Graaf had insisted upon, before Waldo said that they must leave. Olympia bade the little group of friends good-bye and turned round to find Waldo standing behind her. 'You had better wear this,' he told her in a matter-of-fact voice, and helped her into a coat – mink, a rich light brown mink. She wanted to smooth its soft fur and at least take a look at herself in it, but again there was no time. She glanced at him, very elegant in his dark grey suit, but he was looking at Bill Bentinck, smiling at something he was saying; it was hardly the moment to thank him. Amidst a chorus of good-byes, they went out of the house together.

There was a car drawn up to the pavement, a Lamborghini Euraco S, a glorious thing, its cream paintwork spotless. Waldo opened its door and ushered her in and then went round to his own seat. When he had settled himself beside her, she asked breathlessly, 'This car – is it yours?'

'Yes.' He looked at her with a half smile. 'Don't you like it?'

'Not like it?' she echoed. 'It's marvellous – absolutely super,' and before he could start the car: 'Thank you for my lovely coat – I've never had a fur one before.' An obvious remark which he received with the faintest twitch of his lips.

'My wedding present.' His glance flickered over her. 'You look charming, Olympia, and that's a pretty thing on your head. You've done your hair differently, too.'

She drew a deep breath of pure pleasure. 'Oh, thank you – I did hope you might notice – the hairdresser showed me how. I – I wanted to look as nice as possible.'

'And you did – and do,' he assured her as the car purred into life and slid smoothly forward. Olympia turned to wave to the little party on the steps of the house. She would see them all again, she supposed, but she had no idea when. She had no idea about anything much, had she? She thought about it for a moment and somehow it didn't matter.

CHAPTER FOUR

THEY were going, the doctor explained as they threaded their way through London and out on to the motorway to Dover, to cross to Ostend and then drive, in the matter of an hour or so, to Middelburg, and Olympia, who had spent some time poring over a map of Holland while she had been staying with Mrs. van der Graaf, was able to follow his remarks about their journey with no trouble at all. She had never been out of England before and she was wildly excited, but she kept these feelings hidden under a serene face, for it was obvious that Waldo thought nothing of the journey, just as she had thought nothing of the journey by bus down Primrose Hill. The nursing home seemed a long way away now; she had gone back to see the patients, but Aunt Maria had barely spoken to her and then with a spite which had made her wince. She hadn't come to the wedding either, only written a letter warning Olympia of her folly. She had torn it up and then cried a little about it. Perhaps later, when Aunt Maria had got used to the idea, she might not feel so badly about it; indeed, she had no reason to – she hadn't been inconvenienced at all, for Waldo, true to his promise, had found a splendid nurse to take her place, an older woman who got on well with Mrs. Cooper and the others and was very efficient besides. Olympia had wondered where Waldo had found her and hadn't liked to ask. He had said that they were friends, but there had been times when she had found it difficult to talk to him or ask him questions. Doubtless, she thought hopefully, that would come right in time.

But he wasn't being difficult now; he talked pleasantly about the day's happenings as he sent the car down the A1, and once on board the ferry there was so much to see that, her tongue nicely loosened by the lunch they had eaten on the way, Olympia kept up a constant flow of questions and observations, to all of which her companion lent a patient ear, answering her with a charming courtesy although he must surely have found them a little boring. She didn't think of that until afterwards, when they were in the car, tearing along towards Holland and Middelburg. She had fallen silent now, suddenly overcome with fears of the future. Supposing Ria didn't like her, and how about the housekeeper Waldo had mentioned? Supposing she couldn't cope with his household or fit into his life? Supposing his friends disliked her? She became very quiet indeed.

They were over the River Schelde and leaving Vlissingen behind, with the towers and spires of Middelburg before them, only a mile or so away, when Waldo said gently: 'You're a little scared, aren't you? You have no need to be, I promise you; everyone knows that you are coming as my wife and they will be delighted to welcome you and be your friend. Now don't worry.' He cast her a quick, shrewd glance. 'Tea will be nice, won't it?' he asked lightly, and she, feeling better already, agreed quite cheerfully.

Her future home was in the very heart of the small city, almost in the shadow of the great church with its tower – Lange Jan. The house, large and solid and square, flanked by similar dwellings, faced the entrance to the Abdij – the abbey, its twelfth-century buildings, beautifully restored, encircling a large open space which she barely glimpsed from the street. And the street itself was charming with a grass plot in its centre and a scattering of trees, a little backwater of a place and peaceful. That much she was able to see before the doctor stopped the car before his door, helped her out and ushered her into his home.

The hall was narrow with a tiled floor, plain white plastered walls and a splendid ornamental plaster ceiling, its swags of fruit and flowers running riot and spilling down the walls to ornament the tops of the doors. There was a large console table along one wall, on which was a great bowl of spring flowers, and a staircase half-way down the hall, set at right angles to it. There was a passage beside it and a woman came hurrying along it to meet them. She broke into speech as she caught sight of them and the doctor said easily: 'This is my housekeeper, Emma – she speaks no English, but you will find her a treasure and I'm sure you will soon learn something of our language.'

Olympia shook hands and smiled nervously, a smile which Emma returned with a wide welcoming one of her own. She was a short, dumpy little woman with dark hair worn severely in a bun, and very neat in her dress. Olympia suddenly felt at ease with her; language or no language, she thought they might be friends. Emma said something to the doctor, smiled again at Olympia and opened one of the mahogany doors which lined the hall.

'Tea,' said Waldo, his hand under her elbow, 'in the sitting-room. We can go round the house presently.'

The room was warm and welcoming; claret-coloured curtains draped in their satin swathes on either side of the tall windows, matched the silky carpet

61

on the wooden floor. The furniture was large and comfortable, the chairs roomy. There was a sofa facing the chimneypiece, with two chairs on either side, and a scattering of little tables bearing reading lamps and a miscellaneous collection of silver and china. Olympia crossed this pleasing apartment and took the chair the doctor offered. She hadn't known what to expect, but she was delighted to find that her half-formed notions as to Waldo's home had been entirely eclipsed by a quite beautiful reality.

Tea came; delicate china upon a silver tray. She poured out a little clumsily while Waldo, sitting opposite her in a great winged chair, talked placidly about things that didn't matter while she thanked him silently for being so understanding. There were three cups on the tray; she was on the point of asking who was to join them when the door opened and Ria came in. She wasn't in the least like her father; small and dark, with an elfin face lighted by enormous dark eyes and a mop of brown hair brushing her small shoulders. She gave Olympia a hand with wary politeness, and Olympia, understanding the wariness, was careful to be friendly and nothing more. That the child was devoted to her father was evident; she shrilled her delight at seeing him again and giggled happily when he tossed her high before sitting her down on a stool between them. She was a charming child with charming manners; Olympia was enchanted by her even though she took care to sit back quietly and leave father and daughter to talk together.

'You won't mind if we speak Dutch?' he had asked her. 'Ria hasn't started English yet – I daresay she will pick it up quickly enough with you, though.'

He turned back to the small creature and became

immersed in talk once more and presently had drawn Olympia into a three-sided conversation in which he acted as interpreter. It was a little laborious, but they all laughed a good deal and Olympia began to think that getting to know Ria might not be so difficult after all, but when they all got up to tour the house, she was shocked at the look of dislike the little girl threw at her. She told herself that it was natural enough that Ria shouldn't take to her at once; she would have to have patience and go slowly. With Waldo between them they crossed the hall and began their tour of inspection.

The dining-room came first, panelled in grey wood and with a moss green carpet and heavy velvet curtains of the same shade, setting off the mahogany furniture to great advantage. The walls were hung with cream silk and there were a number of charming flower paintings hung around the room. There was a long sideboard too, holding a splendid collection of silver. Olympia, gazing round her, tried to imagine herself sitting at the long table, facing Waldo, guests on either side of them, and her imagination boggled; it was something of a relief to see the small sitting-room at the back of the house, with its french windows opening on to a surprisingly large garden. It was a cosy, well lived in room, with comfortable leather chairs, a great many books on the shelves which lined the walls and a circular table to one side, piled with more books and magazines. There was a games table too and an old-fashioned stove, very ornate with its polished nickel plating. A room in which to sit comfortably and read or write and sew.

The doctor's study was next to it, a smaller room, sparsely furnished and very businesslike, and leading from it, a small surgery. 'I sometimes see patients here,' he explained, 'though most of them come to my consulting rooms on the other side of the Abbey buildings.' He led the way down the hall and up the uncarpeted oak staircase, Ria clinging to his hand. 'You can see the kitchen later on,' he suggested. 'Emma will want to show you round – come and see your room.'

It seemed enormous after her dim and poky bedroom at the nursing home. It was furnished with a restrained luxury which enchanted her; there was a Hepplewhite fourposter against one wall, its draperies of palest pink, and the carpet was a riot of pale roses on a cream ground. The curtains at the two windows were of a deep rose brocade and between them was a delicate rosewood dressing table holding a triple mirror, and to match the polished brown of the furniture, the day-bed was covered in a rich brown velvet, as were the two comfortable chairs on each side of the burnished steel fireplace.

Olympia blinked. 'Is this really my room?' she asked in a small voice.

'All yours. It hasn't been in use for years – it was my mother's, and nothing in it has been changed.'

Not Estelle's then. She felt thankful about that, although she wasn't sure why, but it had been thoughtful of him to tell her.

'There's a bathroom through that door,' he pointed out, 'and on this side there's my dressing-room and my room beyond it and another bathroom. Are you tired, or would you like to see the rest of the house?'

She disclaimed all tiredness; perhaps he was anxious to get the inspection over with, and it wasn't as though they were looking over their new home for the first time. She fetched a small sigh and followed him out of the room.

They inspected more bedrooms; there were a great many of them, but then the house extended back a long way from the street in a most unexpected way. And upstairs, on the floor above, was Ria's room, small, and furnished exactly as a little girl's room should be. Olympia would have loved to have lingered, to examine the toys scattered around and admire the pictures, but one look at the little girl's face decided her against it; Ria didn't want her there, any fool could have seen that. She sighed again and crossed the landing to look into two more rooms and then pause while the doctor explained that the two doors opposite Ria's room were where Emma and Joanna the maid slept. There was a small narrow staircase beside the end door, leading to the attics. 'You can leave those for a wet day,' the doctor suggested, 'they're full of odds and ends, I'm afraid. Emma cleans them out every now and then, but she always puts everything back again, however useless.'

They all went downstairs again, back into the big sitting-room, and the doctor fetched the dolls' house with the suggestion that Ria might be allowed to play with it for an hour before her bedtime before he excused himself on the grounds of telephoning his partners, and disappeared, leaving Olympia and Ria in each other's uneasy company. He had probably forgotten that neither of them could understand the other, and when Olympia made a tentative move to join the little girl on the floor in front of her new toy, she was met with such a bleak look of dislike that she went back to her chair and picked up a paper lying on the table beside it. The paper was, naturally enough, printed in Dutch, which left her with nothing to amuse herself

65

with but her own uncertain thoughts. She remembered her aunt's warning then, and a little niggling doubt crept into her head and would probably have swelled to enormous proportions if the doctor hadn't returned at that moment. He made no comment upon the silence which greeted him, but dropped on his knees beside Ria, saying over his shoulder in a comfortable voice: 'Tomorrow you shall start your Dutch lessons, Olympia – there is an excellent teacher close by. I've just been on the telephone to him, he will come each morning. It won't be long before you can at least acquire a basic Dutch; enough to talk to Emma and Ria and do your shopping, and once you start it will get easier.'

'Is it very difficult?' she asked anxiously.

He smiled nicely. 'Yes – but don't let that worry you. You will be able to manage very well with a handful of sentences to begin with, the rest will come easily enough in time.'

'Yes, but I'm not clever, you know.' She got to her feet. 'I think I'll go and unpack, if you don't mind.' She hesitated. 'Do you want me to do anything about Ria's supper? Who puts her to bed?'

He had risen to his feet too, to come and stand beside her. 'Emma will see to that tonight – tomorrow will be time enough for you to start your new life.' His blue eyes studied her face carefully. 'You must be tired; we seem to have squeezed a great deal into one day, and I haven't even welcomed you to your new home, dear girl.' He bent to kiss her, a friendly, impersonal kiss. 'I hope you will be very happy here.'

Olympia nodded without speaking. Indeed, she had no words for the moment; she was struggling to behave normally, as though nothing had happened, as though she hadn't just discovered that she was very much in love with this cool, quiet man who had married her – as he had been at pains to point out to her – because of the mutual benefits they might share. Only these benefits hadn't included love. And why, after having known him all these weeks, did she have to discover that now? It would have to be a secret, kept for ever and ever . . .

'Do you feel all right?' asked the doctor. 'You look a little pale.'

She might as well begin as she meant to go on: she gave him a serene smile. 'As you say, it's been a long day – not that I'm tired, just a bit excited, that's all. Shall I say good night to Ria now? And if you would tell me what time we have dinner – though I'm sure to be ready before then.'

He spoke easily. 'Of course – I've always dined at half past seven, after evening surgery, if that suits you? Will you come down for a drink about seven? Ria goes to bed at half past six.' He glanced at his watch, 'Emma will be coming for her in half an hour or so – a good idea to say good night now.'

She offered her hand to the little girl because she knew instinctively that Ria didn't want to be kissed; small children couldn't be forced, she knew that, and it might take time, but she would wait with patience until they had got to know each other and Ria liked her a little – had even become fond of her. She was a dear little girl, but perhaps Waldo hadn't prepared her enough about their marriage; even if she didn't remember her own mother, she might be fostering a childish image of her in her small heart, and anyone else trying to oust it would seem an interloper.

Olympia went upstairs to her lovely room and sat

down on the edge of the bed to think. It had all seemed very simple and straightforward in London, but she could see now that things wouldn't be quite what she had imagined. She had been told that Waldo was a rich man, but she hadn't quite taken that in; she hadn't expected this lovely old house filled with treasures, certainly she hadn't expected Ria to dislike her, and most important of all, she hadn't expected to fall in love with her husband.

She wasted a lot of time, just sitting there allowing her thoughts to weave their way to and fro in her head before admitting to herself that they were getting her nowhere, because inevitably they returned to Waldo. She began to unpack, glad to have something to do, and when this was done to her satisfaction she did her hair and face with care, and still in the dress she had worn for their wedding, went downstairs.

The doctor was in the sitting-room, in his mammoth armchair, going through his post; a formidable task, it would appear, for although he had remembered to place a wastepaper basket within reach, he had either forgotten about it or ignored it; it stood empty while the floor around him was piled high with screwed-up envelopes, discarded letters and unopened circulars. To make matters worse he got up from his chair as she entered, sending a cascade of paper to join the rest on the floor.

'What an enormous post,' observed Olympia, and quite forgetting the shyness which had overcome her at the thought of seeing him again, got down on her knees and began to stuff the basket full.

He beamed at her before becoming immersed in a closely-written form. 'Dear girl, what a blessing you will be to me. I never could control my letters and

Juffrouw Bruin – my secretary at the surgery – is on holiday. Three piles,' he instructed her, 'circulars, bills and so forth, and letters.' He returned to his reading and then looked up to say: 'They look the same in any language, but you had better make another pile of the ones you aren't certain about.'

He was quite right; a bill was a bill whether she could understand the language or not, and she was nothing if not efficient. Within a few minutes she had the chaos subdued into neat piles and the waste paper basket piled high, and since he was still immersed in his reading, she went and sat in a small button-backed chair close by. She was naturally a quiet girl and her upbringing had made her even more so; she neither moved nor sighed, examined her nails or fidgeted with her hair. It was quite five minutes before he looked up, cast down his papers and exclaimed: 'Olympia, I had forgotten. Drinks before dinner – will sherry suit you, or a Dubonnet?'

She chose the latter and when he had handed her a glass, asked: 'Is it very interesting? Don't stop reading on my account.'

She smiled a little shyly. 'I don't need to be entertained, you know.'

'I can see that we are going to suit each other very well. This is a report on a patient I sent for open heart surgery – doing rather well, despite complications, too.' He plunged into highly technical details of the case. 'I've been to Utrecht to see her several times. I fancy she's out of the wood now.'

'Young?' Olympia wanted to know.

'Almost twelve. There was no chance to do anything sooner, she's an asthmatic as well, poor child, but happily that is improving.'

'Oh, the poor little girl! Will she go home to convalesce or will you send her to an after-care centre?'

'Send her away, I think. Her father's finances must be stretched to their limit by now, and there's a splendid place not too far away.'

Olympia sipped her drink. Intent on keeping the conversation on safe, impersonal lines, she asked: 'How does your National Health work in Holland – there is one, of course?'

'Oh, yes – but not quite like England; it will take a little explaining. Shall we go into dinner and I can tell you about it while we eat.'

The meal was delicious; Emma, who did the cooking, had a magic touch and there was champagne, presumably to celebrate their wedding day, although the doctor was so engrossed in explaining the *Ziekenfonds* to her that beyond opening the bottle, filling her glass and raising his own to her in an absent-minded fashion, he had probably forgotten all about it. She must be the only girl in the world, she thought wryly, whose husband spent the first few hours of their life together explaining the Health Service of the Netherlands to her. She rather unwisely tossed off the champagne and when he refilled her glass, drank that down too. It certainly lent a more cheerful light to the situation, indeed, she had to fight a tendency to giggle. It was Emma, bearing in a splendid dessert to round off their meal, who brought their rather one-sided conversation to an end. She offered the delectable confection with a little speech and a smile for Olympia, who smiled back, relieved that it might now be possible to change the subject. Seemingly it was; with a brief reminder to her to ask him to finish his explanations some other time, the doctor applied himself to filling glasses once more, and this time Emma and Joanna came and stood by the table and toasted them as well. And when she had served the sweet, the dish was returned to Emma with instructions to finish it in the kitchen in honour of the bride and groom. Olympia, understanding without comprehending a word, said quickly before Emma should go: 'Waldo, please will you tell Emma that the dinner was delicious – she's a wonderful cook and this dessert looks like something out of fairyland.'

He translated rapidly and Emma smiled widely, nodded her head at them both and trotted away. As soon as she had gone, Olympia asked: 'What is it called, this pudding? – it's heavenly.'

'Gateau St. Honoré – made especially in your honour.'

For some stupid reason she wanted to cry. She took a mouthful of the choux pastry instead, and swallowed the threatening tears with it and contrived to say cheerfully, 'How very kind of her, to – to celebrate like that.'

She was instantly sorry that she had said it, for Waldo paused with his fork half-way to his mouth. 'And I haven't celebrated at all, only to bore you unendingly about the Health Service. My dear Olympia, I am sorry . . .'

She interrupted him. 'That wasn't what I meant – I wasn't bored and there is no need to celebrate, is there? I'm very content if you are.'

She had forced her voice to friendly warmth and nothing more, and was rewarded by his smile and his quick: 'I can only repeat that we shall suit each other very well, you and I. And now if you're ready, shall we go into the sitting-room for our coffee? I must tell you about the running of the house and the arrangements I have made for you.'

It was pleasant sitting by the bright fire while she listened in some awe to him telling her about the account he had opened for her. The size of her allowance seemed excessive to her, and she said so, to be told that she would doubtless need all of it and probably more besides. 'We shall go out a good deal,' he explained, 'and now that I have you as a hostess, we shall entertain a great deal more than I have been doing. You will need pretty clothes and hairdressing and so on. There is also a sum of money paid in for Ria. Elisabeth has always bought her clothes, but it will be more satisfactory now that you are here to do it.'

'Who is Elisabeth?' Olympia's voice sounded faint in her own ears; it was quite frightening, the fierceness of her feelings at the mention of another woman – surely she wasn't jealous? She had never had occasion to feel jealousy before and it was a frightening sensation.

'Have I never mentioned her?' he wanted to know carelessly. 'An old friend – we have known each other for fifteen years at least. She was fond of Estelle and naturally enough when she died, Elisabeth helped in every way she could with Ria. She lives close by, you will meet her very soon, I have no doubt.'

Very soon indeed; Emma came in at that moment, looking faintly disapproving and muttered to the doctor, who got up with every sign of pleasure. 'Elisabeth is here now – how providential,' he told Olympia, who found herself disagreeing violently, if silently, with him.

'You're not tired?' He was already on the way to the door and her murmured answer was lost in the sudden outburst of talk as their visitor came in.

And she was such a pretty girl, Olympia saw at once, hating herself for the half-formed hope that Elisabeth might be dumpy and middle-aged. She was neither; she was fair and superbly built, with bright blue eyes and a voice which would have charmed her worst enemy. She gave the doctor her hand with the briefest of greetings and came across the room to Olympia. 'You must think me a very rude woman,' she said in English, 'calling at this hour of the evening and on the first night of your arrival in your new home, but I am as a sister to Waldo and I have so much wanted to meet you.'

She smiled with such obvious pleasure that Olympia found herself smiling back, her first doubts stilled. Elisabeth might be gorgeously pretty, but she was nice too – and an old friend. Perhaps she would become her friend too.

She stayed only a very short while; presently she bade them good night in her soft voice, expressing a wish to help Olympia in whatever way she could and saying that she would come again in the morning, and when the doctor came back into the room after seeing her to the door, Olympia said impulsively: 'What a very nice person Elisabeth is, and how pretty. Surely she's married?'

He shook his head. 'She's had offers enough, but she's very happy as she is, I believe. She lives very much as she wishes; her father died some years ago and she lives with her mother, but she's always been allowed to go her own way – in any case, it would take an exceptional man to take her fancy.'

Waldo was an exceptional man, thought Olympia

worriedly; they would have made a strikingly handsome pair, too; it seemed strange that he hadn't married Elisabeth, but perhaps she had refused him? – had she not said that she felt like a sister to him? – and she had behaved towards him like one, too, nor had there been anything in his manner towards her . . . She suddenly longed for her bed as she fought the terrible suspicion that she might have bitten off more than she could chew.

'You wouldn't mind if I went to bed?' she asked the doctor. 'I know it's still quite early . . .'

'My dear, of course – it's been a long day, hasn't it? I think I'll catch up on some reading for an hour or so. This is the best time of the day for it – the house is quiet and there is no one to disturb me.'

A strong hint for future evenings? she wondered peevishly as she wished him a good night. He had gone to the door with her and held it open for her to go through, but he didn't kiss her good night.

In her room presently, brushing her hair before the mirror, she assured her reflection that she hadn't expected him to, anyway. Her face stared back at her with sad eyes and a mouth which trembled a little. She turned her back upon it, and clad in one of the exquisite nighties which Mrs. van der Graaf had cajoled her into buying, jumped into bed.

She wakened early and lay wondering if she should get up. She felt very much a guest in the house, which was foolish, she knew; she should have asked about it before she had gone to bed. But she need not have worried, for only a few seconds after the carillons of Middelburg had chimed their chorus for seven o'clock, there was a knock on the door, and Joanna came in with morning tea, a luxury Olympia had done without until she had gone to stay with Aunt Betsy. She was sitting up in bed sipping it when there was another tap on the door – this time the doctor. His good morning was cheerful and matter-of-fact, his glance brief and oblivious of the nightie. She was surprised to see that he was already dressed, something she commented upon, glad of something to say.

'Were you called out?'

'No – surgery starts at half past eight, though, and until recently I had a dog to walk before breakfast, so getting up early has become a habit.'

'A dog – what happened to him?'

'He died, he was elderly and had a heart condition, but I had him for twelve years – one gets attached.'

He was standing looking out of the window, with his back to her. She said with quick sympathy, 'Oh, I'm sorry, but could you not get another one in his place – he must have left a gap.'

'Now that you are here, I don't see why not. You see, there was the question of training a puppy and I'm so often not home. It would hardly be fair to leave him to Emma and Joanna.'

He turned round at last and she put down her cup and spoke before she could stop herself. 'Waldo, please may we have a dog? I don't mind looking after him and training him when you're not home, in fact, I should like it very much – I never had a dog, you know – and Ria would like it, I'm sure.'

He took the tea tray from her knee and sat down on the edge of the bed. 'You would? Then we will have one. Large or small?'

'I don't mind. Ria does like dogs, I suppose?'

'Very much. There is a cat who lives with Emma in the kitchen; she's a great friend of his, but I know she prefers dogs.' He got to his feet. 'We'll see about it, let me see – I'll telephone someone who might know of a puppy, it should be easy enough. Are you coming down to breakfast? It's in half an hour or so, but if you would rather have yours later, you only have to say so.'

'I'll come down and have it with you and Ria.' He was almost at the door. 'Waldo, does she go to school?'

He turned at her question. 'Good lord, didn't I tell you? I'm unpardonably forgetful. Yes, she goes to morning school, that's why I thought you might like to have your Dutch lessons then – while she's there. I drop her off on the way to the surgery.'

He nodded in a friendly fashion and went away, and when next she saw him he was sitting at the breakfast table, going through his post and answering Ria's insistent piping voice with great patience. Olympia wished the little girl good morning and tried not to see the lowering look she was accorded while she poured coffee for herself and buttered a roll. There was little need for her to talk, though. Ria kept up a ceaseless chatter, and the doctor, while maintaining a casual conversation between the perusal of his letters, didn't seem to expect her to answer at great length. He got up to go presently, taking Ria with him, and she was left to herself and feeling a little lost. There were surely things she should be doing about the house – make the beds for instance? or clear the table, and was she supposed to go to the kitchen and see Emma? She decided to do that.

Joanna was washing up at the sink and Emma was writing in a small book at the kitchen table. She got up as Olympia went in, smiling and pulling forward a chair and then pointing to the book. A shopping list presumably, but who was to do the shopping? Olympia was pondering the best way of finding this out when the front door bell rang and Joanna went to answer it. It was barely nine o'clock and Olympia hadn't expected to have visitors quite so early in the morning, but she was really glad to see Elisabeth follow Joanna into the kitchen.

'I beg your pardon for coming into your kitchen as though it were my own,' Elisabeth cast her an apologetic glance, 'but I have done it many times before, you understand? I forget. I thought that you might want help.'

'Oh, I do,' said Olympia with relief. 'You have no idea how glad I am to see you; I don't know what I'm supposed to do.' She waved a small capable hand round her rather vaguely.

The other girl laughed gently. 'How bad of Waldo to tell you nothing,' she exclaimed in her soft gentle voice. 'Is that not like a man? and you do not speak our language. You do not mind if I talk with Emma?'

'Go ahead.' Olympia felt relieved but somehow lonely as she listened to their meaningless conversation. It was better when Elisabeth said at last: 'Emma says that you do not need to do anything in the house, unless you wish to do so, she and Joanna have always done everything between them. She says it would be nice if you saw to the flowers, and that you will be busy with your lessons each morning and there is Ria to fetch home from school each morning at noon. And presently there will be visitors and friends who will call. She will be most glad to go around the house with you and show you the cupboards and drawers, and if you like to go to the shops with her, she will be happy to teach you what to buy and how much it costs.'

Olympia heaved a sigh of pleasure. 'Oh, that's nice – I shall like that, to know a little about things. Will you tell Emma I'd love to go with her. I'll get my teacher to explain the money to me today; that will be a start.'

Elisabeth nodded. 'That's right, and before long you will know enough Dutch to be able to order the meals and so on. There are foods which Waldo does not like, and those which he likes very much, and I will tell you of those – and Ria too, she is perhaps a little awkward sometimes, but I am sure that very soon she will like you very much and that will be nice for all of you.'

Olympia frowned. 'She doesn't like me at all at the moment; I'm sorry about it, but I quite understand that I'm a stranger to her, and she has no reason to like me, has she? I'm quite prepared to wait until she is used to me.'

Elisabeth tucked a friendly arm into hers. 'You will do very well, Olympia, and remember that I am always glad to help you. Waldo is a busy man, and besides that, he has left everything in Emma's hands for such a long time – even when Estelle was alive she had no interest in the house, you see – if there were parties or entertaining, I saw to them for her.'

Olympia was momentarily diverted; she hadn't imagined Waldo's wife like that at all; he must have loved her very much not to have minded such an arrangement; perhaps she had been so beautiful that he hadn't cared, perhaps all that mattered to him was to come home to some cherished, fragile creature who was his whole world. She realized that her imagination was running riot and that it hurt.

She cheered up later, though, for her teacher, Mijnheer Blom, was a youngish man full of confidence in his ability to teach her the rudiments of his language in the quickest possible time, and some of this confidence he transmitted to her, so that by the end of her first lesson she had mastered a handful of useful words, counted to ten, learned the money, and could say a tolerable good morning, good evening and how do you do. What was more, he promised her that within a week she would have enough words at her command to make herself understood in her own kitchen, and when she inquired, rather apprehensively, about the grammar, he urged her warmly to forget that for the moment. As he got up to go, he said hearteningly, 'Tomorrow we will walk round this house and I will tell you the Dutch word for everything which we see in it; we shall do that every day until you are able to tell me, and not I you – in that way you will learn very quickly.'

Olympia was left with her homework and an over-powering desire to learn all she could in the quickest way possible, and when it was time to fetch Ria from school she boldly refused Joanna's company, and armed with a street map with the school marked with a cross upon it, set off by herself. It was a pleasant day, though cool, and she found her surroundings de-lightful. She had discovered that the peaceful little place in which they lived was called Balans and led into a fairly busy street. She turned into it and walked along slowly, picking out the names of the side streets as she went. The school was down a narrow cul-de-sac and the children were already coming out. She saw Ria almost immediately with a bunch of little boys and girls of her own age, and waited quietly until the child saw her, but if she had hoped for an improvement in Ria's manner towards her, she was disappointed. The child scowled, bade her small companions good-bye and came slowly towards her.

Olympia took a reluctant little hand. 'Hullo,' she said cheerfully, and then in her very experimental Dutch: '*Wij gaan naar huis*,' which at least had the effect of making Ria giggle at her funny accent and burst into childish speech which Olympia was quite unable to understand.

Ria fell silent presently, and so, perforce, did Olympia, so that the short journey back home was hardly a happy one. They didn't talk over their lunch either, although Olympia tried pointing to the things around them and saying the English, in the hope that Ria would copy her – but Ria was either not interested or unfriendly, she wasn't sure which. And their afternoon walk together was just as silent; they went through the Abbey grounds and out through the other gate into the town and looked at a few shops, then walked home again the same way.

Not a very successful day, thought Olympia as she tidied herself for tea after attending to the little girl's small needs. It was a relief when the doctor came home in the evening, very soon after tea, to find the pair of them sitting by the fire, Ria engrossed in the dolls' house and Olympia thumbing through her dictionary. No doubt they presented a pleasing picture to him, thought Olympia, her heart racing at the sight of him – if only he knew what a miserable day they had spent! But here common sense came to her aid; nothing was to be gained by self-pity; it was early days yet, there was no reason why Ria and she shouldn't become firm friends in due course. For that matter there was no reason why Waldo, aided no doubt by some miracle, shouldn't discover himself in love with her. She smiled wryly at her thoughts and asked him in a nice friendly voice what sort of a day he had had.

But she was forced to admit to herself later that for the moment he showed no signs of falling in love. They had spent a pleasant evening; an hour or so with Ria before she had put the little girl to bed, and then another quiet hour before dinner, talking in a matter-of-fact way about the day's happenings – just like an old married couple, she thought wistfully. And after dinner he had excused himself on the grounds of work to be done, and gone to his study. She had tapped on the door on her way to bed at half past ten and he had wished her a good night with the casual warmth of an old friend. She went upstairs uphappily, despite the strong reminder to herself that his behaviour was exactly what she had expected; it was exactly as it had been before they married – good friends, he had said, only she had been foolish enough to spoil it all by falling in love with him.

CHAPTER FIVE

A WEEK went by at the end of which Olympia had, just as the redoubtable Mijnheer Blom had assured her, acquired a fair number of useful words in the Dutch language, a handful of convenient phrases, and a good slice of his buoyant self-confidence. She had also acquired an even deeper love for Waldo, who was proving himself to be kind, placidly good-humoured and generous to a fault. She had been taken aback at the size of the allowance he had given her, but over and above that, when they had gone out with Ria one afternoon, he had bought her several expensive trifles she had admired, and would have gone on doing this if she hadn't realized in time that she had only to say that she liked something for him to immediately purchase it for her. And when she had pointed out that she already had a generous allowance from him and he had no need to buy her anything, he had replied that after years of being alone but for Ria, it was a pleasure to have a wife for whom he might buy pretty things. This remark had increased her self-confidence still further; she found a good hairdresser and arranged to visit him weekly, and took even greater pains with her face, while at the back of her mind a resolve was forming that she would make him love her. She wasn't at all sure how to set about this, for she had had little experience with men – Aunt Maria had seen to that – but looking at her reflection in the great gilt-framed mirror on the landing she took courage from it; pretty clothes, a good hairdresser and the knowledge that she had

begun to master the Dutch language and all its intri-
cacies had all contributed towards turning her into a
quite different girl from the one she had been – the one
Waldo had, rather surprisingly, chosen to marry.
What could he have seen in her? she wondered; she
must have looked pretty awful – she remembered the
tweed suit and shuddered.

And as the days went by, she began to take her place
in the household, although she had felt nervous enough
when he had mentioned one evening that he had accepted an invitation to dinner from one of his partners.
'Wim Cassells,' he told her. 'You'll like him and his
wife Netta.' He glanced at her with a kindly smile.
'They have been longing to meet you, but they thought
you would need a little time to get used to everything
first. Paul Bos, my other partner, will be there too. He's
the youngest of us and has only been married a couple
of years. His wife is about your age, I should imagine –
she's Emmeline, but everyone calls her Emmy.' He had
got up and strolled over to pour their drinks. 'Do you
want a new dress for the occasion?'

She was quite shocked. 'I've several dresses I've not
yet worn at all. Shall I have to dress up, do you suppose?'

His lips twitched, but he answered her gravely. 'No,
something pretty – like that green thing you had on the
other evening.'

Olympia couldn't stop herself smiling; she hadn't
thought that he had noticed what she wore. 'It's cashmere,' she told him. 'I'll wear it.'

They had started a little late for their dinner party,
though, because Ria had chosen to be difficult. In the
ten days or so in which Olympia had lived in the house,
she had begun, very gingerly, to change the little girl's

routine. It had been easy enough to take over from Emma in the mornings, helping with shoelaces and difficult buttons and brushing hair, and the morning walk home from school each morning had become a settled matter over which the little girl no longer pouted. Indeed, Olympia hoped that she was even beginning to enjoy it a little, for now they could talk just a little. The afternoon walk had been harder to establish, but with the gentle bribe of two hours in which to play with the dolls' house when they got back home, that too had been dealt with. But bedtime was another matter; Ria disliked going to bed at a reasonable hour. Even the offer of eating her supper in the little sitting-room while the doctor and Olympia sat there too, talking over the day in a pleasant fashion, wasn't enough to persuade her. And when Olympia had mentioned it to Waldo, unfortunately at a time when he was frowning over some hospital reports, he had dismissed her uneasiness lightly and with faint impatience.

'My dear girl,' he had said, 'I warned you that Ria was difficult and rather out of hand. I'm sure you are doing very well with her, and do remember that Elisabeth has been giving in to her far too much and I, I'm ashamed to admit, have always been too busy. Now you mention it, she has been staying up far too late in the evening. I leave it to you to improve matters.'

She had wanted to answer him back, for it seemed to her a little unfair that she should be the scapegoat for someone else's indulgence. Elisabeth was a dear, but so gentle and kind, and probably it had never entered her head to refuse Ria anything. And that particular evening Ria had been particularly trying. There had been floods of tears and faces pulled, small heels drummed on the carpeted floor and torrents of Dutch which Olympia was thankful she couldn't understand. Waldo had come home in the middle of it all and had come upstairs to the bathroom to see what all the noise was about. Olympia, soaked from Ria's angry splashings in the bath, looked up to find him standing in the door-way, and although he wasn't smiling, she was aware that he was amused. She gave him an austere frown, whisked the little girl out of the bath, wrapped her in a towel and said cheerfully, 'Here's Papa.'

It was the signal for a fresh outburst of tears. Olym-pia, always a practical girl, pulled forward a stool, waved an invitation to the doctor to sit on it, hoisted her cross burden on to his knee and said forthrightly: 'The poppet is full of grievances – will you dry her and let her unburden herself? I'll be back in a minute with her nightie, then if you would carry her down to the sitting-room – she likes that, you know – I'll have her supper ready by the fire. Can you spare the time to stay with her? She's had enough of me for the moment.'

His large, well-kept hands were already busy with the towel. 'That sounds like a good idea. Yes, of course I can spare the time, though I was hoping to spend it with you, but never mind that now. Perhaps we shall have time for a talk after we get back this evening.'

Her whole being glowed with the knowledge that he wanted her company. 'Do you want a drink?' she asked.

He turned his head to look at her and smiled slowly. 'What a thoughtful wife – yes, dear girl, I do. I'll have it downstairs while this imp is having her supper.'

The delay had been worth it too. Ria poured out her small woes, was dried, put into her nightie and dressing gown, reproved gently and borne downstairs on the doctor's shoulder, to eat her supper in his company. By the time Olympia returned to take her to bed she had recovered a good deal of her spirits, and beyond some half-hearted grumbling as she was tucked up for the night, appeared to welcome the truce between them, however uneasy. Olympia had had to hurry after that in order to be ready for the dinner party, but she managed it with a minute or two to spare, and no one seeing her coming slowly down the stairs would have guessed that her serene appearance covered a variety of worries and damped-down unhappiness which was somehow all part and parcel of her love for the doctor.

After that bad beginning, though, the evening had been a success, and what was more, she had enjoyed herself enormously. For one thing, everyone spoke English, which made her feel instantly at home, and Waldo was everything she could have wished, charming and courteous and attentive, and yet she had to admit to herself, she could detect nothing more than his usual friendliness towards her – hardly the attitude of a newly married man, but more as though they had been a comfortably married couple of some years' standing. But there was no use in letting that worry her, indeed she would have to make up her mind to nothing more than that for the rest of their lives together, unless by some miracle she should succeed in making him fall in love with her. Her mouth curved at the thought and she glanced up to find his gaze fixed on her – an admiring gaze; even she, inexperienced though she was, could see that. She looked away, bursting with her small triumph, wondering why the admiration had been tinged with surprise.

They returned rather late, for they had sat around talking after dinner and it was eleven o'clock before they left Wim's home on the other side of Middelburg. Olympia went into the quiet house while Waldo put the car away, and wandered into the sitting-room where a lamp had been left burning. He joined her there in a few minutes and asked her at once if she was tired.

'No, not at all,' she assured him. 'What a very pleasant evening.'

'You enjoyed it? I'm glad.' He was standing just inside the door, watching her. 'I hoped you would; we see a good deal of each other, Wim and Paul and I, and that means that our wives meet frequently, too.'

'That will be nice,' said Olympia in a rather small voice. 'I've never had many friends – I shall like it very much.'

He sauntered towards her. 'You're not lonely, Olympia? You're happy here?'

'No, I'm not lonely and I'm very happy,' she told him steadily.

He was close now, close enough to put his hands on her shoulders. 'I have a day free on Saturday, so I thought we might go out, the three of us – I have a friend, Gijs van Amstel, who has a practice in Zierikzee – that's a little town near here. He married an English girl a year or so ago, a charming creature – they're expecting their first baby very soon. They want us for lunch, would you like that?'

She smiled widely. 'Oh, very much, Waldo, and so will Ria. Do we go by car?'

He nodded. 'Half an hour. There is something else I promised you – a puppy. I've arranged to collect him on Sunday, after church.'

Her eyes were on his, and the kindness in them made her blink back sudden tears; it was somehow ironic that this man whom she loved so very much should be the one to make her life so pleasant; all the things she had longed for and dreamed of he had given her with the casual kindness of a big brother.

'You're so kind, Waldo.' Even as she uttered it she heard her voice ascending into a small wail and felt his hands tighten on her shoulders.

'My dear good girl, there is nothing to cry about; I'm not in the least kind – I wanted to see Gijs anyway, and as for the puppy, I must thank you for asking me to get one, it was something I have been putting off.' He bent and kissed her gently. 'You look very pretty this evening, dear girl,' he ran a finger down one cheek, 'and you aren't as thin as you were. When I first met you you were nothing but a small bag of bones.'

She managed: 'Oh, was I?' still thinking of his kiss. 'I mustn't get any plumper, though; none of my clothes will fit.'

'Then we will buy new ones.' He gave her a charming smile. 'Go to bed, my dear.' He bent his head to kiss her once more, barely brushing her hair this time. 'Sleep well.'

She went to bed in a little glow of delight; Waldo had said that she was pretty – he had never told her that before. She curled up in the centre of the wide bed and slept on the thought.

Saturday was a fine clear day, though there was a cold wind blowing. Olympia, in a pretty blue tweed suit she hadn't worn before, her hair piled as the hair-dresser had instructed her, felt a spark of satisfaction at the sight of herself in her mirror; she would never be a raving beauty, but with her soft brown tresses becomingly arranged and her face carefully made up, she could almost pass for pretty, and indeed when she went downstairs for breakfast with Ria holding her hand, friendly for once, the long considered look Waldo gave her was all the confirmation she needed of this pleasant fact.

They set out as soon as the meal was over, with Ria electing to sit in the back of the car with a doll for company; she had wanted to sit beside Waldo, but his firm refusal had squashed that, and when Olympia had offered to keep her company on the back seat, she had been refused with stony politeness and a bleak, polite little face which had almost spoilt the morning for her. But not quite; it was impossible not to feel happy, the prospect of a whole day in Waldo's company saw to that.

She was enchanted by her first glimpse of Zierikzee; the sight of the ancient little town as Waldo slowed the car to go through the centuries-old gate into its main street was eye-catching as well as unexpected. The sun shone on the canal water, the cobbled streets on either side of it were teeming with all the bustle of a Saturday morning, and the houses lining the canal on either side were so varied and picturesque that she didn't know where to look first.

'Like it?' asked Waldo, going slowly along the canal and then crossing it by a bridge at its end. 'Gijs lives just here.' He drew up as he spoke before a large house, rather like his own, only this one had a garden at its side and a wing overlooking it. Olympia had time to see that before the door was opened by an elderly woman. 'Lien, the housekeeper,' Waldo introduced her, said something to make her smile, bade the excited Ria behave herself, and marshalled his small party into the long hall. There were double doors on one side of it; they were thrown open at that moment and Gijs and

Serena van Amstel came out to welcome them. In the general hubbub of chatter which followed, Olympia had a chance to take stock of her host and hostess; Gijs, she decided at once, was nice, large and placid and good-natured, and Serena was quite lovely with a dark, gipsy-like beauty which Olympia envied even as she decided that she was going to like her very much. Their greetings over, Serena said gaily: 'Come upstairs and leave your things – Ria too. The men will start talking shop at any moment; we'll give them ten minutes to get the worst of it off their chests.'

They climbed the stairs at the back of the hall and Olympia said impulsively: 'This is fun – I mean, having an English girl to talk to.'

Serena turned to look at her. 'Have you met Netta and Emmy? Nice, aren't they? but I know what you mean.' She smiled engagingly. 'I would have come down to Middleburg to see you, only I'm hindered by this . . .' she patted herself gently. 'Gijs has lovely old-fashioned ideas about taking care of me, and that means he doesn't like me driving my little Mini – so I don't.'

She led the way into a finely furnished bedroom where she helped Ria with her coat and tidied her hair while Olympia made the best of herself at the mirror, listening to the two of them talking. Serena's Dutch sounded wonderful and she said so.

'Yours will be just as good in no time at all,' her hostess assured her. 'Are you having lessons? And going shopping helps enormously – the thing is to blunder along and never mind tenses and things like that; everyone's far too sweet to laugh at you and in a couple of months you'll be able to hear your own mistakes and put them right.'

'The grammar . . .?'

'Don't bother with it,' counselled Serena airily. 'That will come later – you should have heard me when I started. Do you chat with Ria?'

'A little . . .'

'Difficult, is she? Not to be wondered at – no mother for all that time and only Elisabeth de Val spoiling her.' She looked at Ria, standing on tiptoe to look in the mirror. 'She's a poppet, though.'

'Oh, yes, and I'm very fond of her. Elisabeth's been very kind and helped me a great deal. I think I should have been lost without her during the first few days – she knew everything.'

'I'm sure she did. Shall we go down and prise those men apart? They've probably gone to the surgery to read each other extracts from the *Lancet*.'

But the men were waiting for them, the coffee tray ready on one of the tables in the comfortable sitting-room. From then on the day could be nothing but a success; Ria, borne away by Lien to the kitchen to drink her milk, returned presently with Gus, Serena's dachshund, clasped to her small chest. 'Dog,' she declared importantly, and smiled widely, and having secured an audience, elaborated with: 'A little dog.'

'Oh, you clever girl!' cried Olympia. At least here was something she had achieved with Ria. She looked across the room at Waldo and smiled delightedly and he said lazily: 'You'll have to look to your laurels, Olympia, or Ria will beat you to the language stakes.'

He picked up the little girl and sat her on his knee, Gus and all, and smiled at her over the dark head, so that she glowed once more with content and for the next few hours she lived in an illusion of happiness, helped perhaps by the undoubted bliss of the van

Amstels, as well as Waldo's air of relaxed pleasure; even Ria seemed to accept her at last. The hours passed too quickly; it seemed no time at all before they were getting into the car again with a sleepy, contented little girl safely tucked up on the back seat, the prospect of future visits lightening the uncertainty of Olympia's mood, for she discovered that once they had left the van Amstels, Waldo had become very quiet, and after one or two abortive attempts at conversation, she had allowed her thoughts to take over, wondering what had gone wrong; everything had been absolutely wonderful, but now, all at once, he had become withdrawn, just as though she had annoyed him in some way. She got out of the car in a defiant mood when they reached the house, and followed by Waldo with the sleepy Ria, went indoors, where she was kept busy for the next hour, getting the little girl ready for bed and seeing to her supper.

There was still half an hour till dinner when she eventually got downstairs and the sitting-room was empty, and when she went along to the kitchen Emma told her smiling that there was nothing to do. She went back to the sitting-room and wandered round, moving things and putting them back again, switching the T.V. on and then off. She was choosing a record when Waldo came in.

'I didn't know you were down,' he remarked pleasantly. 'I was in the study.'

'Working?' she spoke for something to say. 'You have a great deal to do.'

'Not more than I can manage – and this isn't work.' He didn't tell her what it was, only offered her a drink and began to talk casually about their day. He talked throughout dinner too, amusing small talk which re-

quired little or no reply from her, only when she met
his eyes from time to time she was disconcerted at their
intentness, so that she found herself asking: 'Waldo,
why were you so – so silent on the way home? Have I
annoyed you? I thought the day was so delightful . . .'

'It was. If I was quiet it was because I had something
to think about – and you never annoy me, dear girl.'

It was extraordinary how he never quite answered
her questions, so that even now she had no idea what
he meant. They went back to the sitting-room for their
coffee and presently, unable to bear staying there with
him any longer without bursting out with her doubts
and fears and love, she pleaded tiredness and said that
she would go to bed. But as she stood up he came over
to her and caught her gently by the arms. 'There's
something I want to say,' he began. 'I'm not quite sure
how to say it because it's something I'm not sure about
myself, but perhaps together . . . will you stay for a few
minutes?'

She stared up at him; she had no idea what he
wanted to talk about, but he was looking at her with
that curious intentness again, as though he were trying
to discover something in her face – some secret. She
had no secrets – but of course she had, an enormous
one, never to be told. She managed a smile. 'Of course
I'll stay – tell me what . . .' but got no further, for the
front door bell pealed and they heard Emma's brisk
step in the hall. But Waldo still held her fast. Only
when the door was opened and Emma's voice said
flatly: 'Juffrouw de Val, Mevrouw,' and Elisabeth
came in, did he release her, and then slowly. His voice
held nothing but pleasure as he greeted Elisabeth,
though, and Olympia hastened to exclaim: 'How nice

to see you – I'll get some more coffee, you must have a cup.'

Elisabeth looked apologetically at her. 'Olympia, I'm so sorry – to call at such an hour and uninvited. Please forgive me, I am not yet used to . . .' She paused and went on diffidently: 'Until you came, I walked in and out as though this were my home and I do not always remember – I am truly sorry.' She looked so upset that Olympia gave her a quick comforting kiss.

'You're always welcome here, you know that. Now I'm going to get that coffee.'

When she got back ten minutes later the two of them were at a table, a great many papers spread out before them, deep in talk. Olympia poured the coffee, set it near them and went back to her chair. After ten minutes or so she got up again and went to the small secretaire in one corner of the room and started to write a quite unnecessary letter. It gave her something to do and made her feel less lonely.

It was half an hour before Waldo turned round to say: 'Sorry about this, Olympia, but Elisabeth has some business she couldn't deal with and she knew I would be home at this time. We shan't be much longer.'

Olympia murmured in a cheerful voice and began on another letter. She wrote without haste, but even so, she had it finished long before Waldo started to tidy up the papers which covered the table. 'That settles that,' he observed cheerfully. 'Elisabeth, I should go along and get these dealt with as soon as you can.'

Elisabeth thanked him in her soft voice. 'I've spoilt your evening,' she declared. 'I feel so mean. Why not come over tomorrow evening for a drink after dinner, just to show there's no hard feelings?'

She spoke to Olympia but looked at Waldo. Olympia looked too. He didn't seem to dislike the idea, so she accepted with a bright smile which most successfully disguised her disappointment. Elisabeth was a dear, but if they went out tomorrow evening there would be no time to talk. She felt annoyed with Waldo for accepting when he could so easily have made some excuse; perhaps he had had second thoughts about telling her whatever it was he had wanted her to know, and anyway, she thought crossly, he wasn't going to get the chance now. Waldo had gone out to the street to see Elisabeth into her car; Olympia took care to be going upstairs as he came in again. From half-way up she turned to smile at him. 'Good night,' she called, 'I did enjoy my day.' She didn't wait to hear his reply but ran up the rest of the stairs and into her room.

Sunday was largely Ria's day, and Olympia, remembering her own bleak childhood, understood this and agreed with it wholeheartedly. Sunday was a family day; however busy Waldo was during the week, unless he was on call, it was Ria's right to have the lion's share of him. She quite cheerfully took a back seat, only making sure that the household ran smoothly, that there was a suitable festive tea if any of Ria's small friends should come round to play, and that she was properly dressed and in good time for church in the morning. Waldo, she had discovered, was an unobtrusive pillar of his church and had taken it for granted that she would be too. And indeed she had been glad of this; at the nursing home she had seldom had the opportunity of going to church on a Sunday, for Aunt Maria, who set great store on presenting the right image to her world, attended regularly, which meant that Olympia had to stay in charge of the patients.

She put on the tweed suit again, adding a pretty little hat, the price of which still made her feel faint, elegant gloves and a handbag which matched her shoes, a combination she had always longed to achieve before her marriage and had never quite managed. She tucked away a stray end of hair, marvelling as she did so how easily it was to get used to having enough money, although she still wasn't quite used to getting the charming gifts Waldo gave her – flowers, a scarf, a beautiful coral and gold brooch which he told her had been in his family for years. She was wearing it now on the jacket of her suit, but he probably wouldn't notice that she had it on and she felt shy of bringing it to his notice, for she had the uneasy feeling that although he gave her so much, he did it as a friend would give; to give her pleasure but not from any deeper feeling on his part.

They walked the short distance to church, through the Abbey courtyard and out the other side, Ria between them, holding their hands, chattering like a small magpie and proud of herself in her best coat. And after church they went home to coffee and then got into the car – the second car Waldo kept in the garage behind the house, a Daimler double six VP, and this time Ria was squeezed between them.

The puppy was a Welsh collie, still small and woolly and endearingly anxious to love and be loved. They made the return journey with Ria on the back seat this time, her arms round the puppy's neck, and the rest of the morning was taken up with choosing a name for him, although it was a foregone conclusion that Ria's insistence that he should be called St. Nikolaas would overrule the more sensible suggestions put forward by her elders. It was the doctor who convinced her finally that the noble-sounding name could be shortened very nicely to Niko, a suggestion which was happily received, and the rest of the day was occupied most satisfactorily in introducing Niko to his new home.

Olympia, watching the little girl playing in the garden with her new companion felt the same illusion as she had had at the van Amstels' house; on the surface everything was so exactly right, and yet she felt uneasily that she was there under false pretences. True, she was managing to establish herself; Emma and Joanna liked her, she had several friends and a number of acquaintances, and when they dined out she could not fail to see the pleased look on Waldo's face whenever he looked at her – sometimes she thought it had been more than pleased – proud would have been the better word; she had basked in that look of his and yet still she didn't quite fit in; countless small things showed up her ignorance of a comfortably run household; she would never, she felt sure, get used to being a rich man's wife, even though Elisabeth, when she had been extra silly about something, pointed out in her kind way that over the years she would become accustomed to her new way of life. 'You do very well,' she had encouraged her, 'and you work so hard at it, too – but not too hard, Olympia. You don't want Waldo to see that – it would irritate him, you know, to see that you are not quite – quite . . . men are strange.'

And as the days passed she thought of that whenever she looked up and found him looking at her with that intense inquiring look. Perhaps he was regretting his marriage, perhaps he was comparing her with Estelle, who must have been the right sort of wife for him; lovely and used to luxury and servants and doing very little all day. She tried to stifle the disturbing thought in hours of homework for Mijnheer Blom, who became quite alarmed at her industry and begged her not to overwork. She was making progress now, though, learning with a fierce concentration, so that she could go shopping by herself and answer the telephone without becoming panic-stricken. She had even engaged Elisabeth's mother in conversation when they had gone round for drinks. Mevrouw de Val spoke almost no English and had been delighted when Olympia understood at least part of what she was saying and could even reply after a fashion, although her replies were a little vague; Elisabeth had carried Waldo off to the greenhouse to see some plants she was worried about, and Olympia was appalled at the strength of her desire to get up and go with them. She was bitterly ashamed of herself when they came back later, because Elisabeth was carrying a bowl of hyacinths which, she explained in her pretty way, were especially for her dear Olympia. Olympia buried her sensible little nose in their fragrance; she had never felt so mean in all her life.

It was three days later – and happy days they had been, too, with the puppy to occupy her as well as looking after a small girl who seemed at last to be more friendly. She had made marmalade too, and done some baking under the motherly eye of Emma; the only small cloud in her sky had been the fact that Waldo hadn't made any attempt to continue the talk which Elisabeth had interrupted. He had been busy, with an epidemic of measles in the town and a series of lectures to give in Utrecht, she would have to have patience with him as well as with his little daughter. But now this morning, he had left the house for his surgery, taking Ria with him as usual, and she had spent half an hour at the store cupboard with Emma deciding the day's meals, but now that this little task was done, there was still a little time before Mijnheer Blom would arrive. She strolled from the kitchen to the small sitting-room, just in time to take the receiver from its cradle as the telephone rang. Answering it was still something of an adventure; sometimes it was one of her ever-widening circle of friends, or one of the partners with a message for Waldo, sometimes it was a patient and she was forced to call Emma. She said now in her careful Dutch, 'Goed Morgen, met Docteur van der Graaf.'

The voice at the other end was unmistakably English, feminine and flustered. 'Do you understand English?' it wanted to know. 'I must speak to Doctor van der Graaf privately – it is very urgent. Would you fetch him for me, please?'

'Would his wife do?' asked Olympia, curiosity quite overcoming her.

The voice – a very pretty voice it was too – became even more agitated. 'No, no – on no account must you tell her, she mustn't know that I'm telephoning.'

Olympia drew a steadying breath and swallowed the questions she longed to ask; instead she inquired sedately: 'Has the doctor your number? If so I'll ask him to ring back when he comes in.'

'Please,' said the voice, 'and you do understand that no one else must know – especially his wife.'

'Oh, yes, I understand,' said Olympia, still sedate. 'Good-bye.' She hung up, a prey to a variety of strong feelings. Who could it be? A lovely voice, belonging, no doubt, to a lovely girl who wanted, for some reason, to talk to Waldo. She remembered uneasily that he had been spending a lot of time in his study lately and

99

several times he had asked that he shouldn't be disturbed because he was expecting an important telephone call – from this girl? There must be some perfectly innocent reason. Common sense took over for a brief moment, but was swamped in a sea of highly imaginative conjectures. If the reason had been an innocent one, why hadn't the girl given her a message for Waldo, and why had she been so anxious that no one should know about the call? Olympia walked up and down the sitting-room, nibbling her fingers and frowning heavily; she was still at it when Mijnheer Blom arrived and remarked playfully that it was evident from her distraught air that she hadn't done her homework.

'Oh, but I have,' she assured him in an over-bright voice. 'The past tense, wasn't it? Look, I know all the verbs you told me to learn.'

She recited them like a good child and he applauded her, wondering at the same time why she looked so pale. She was, he had confided to his wife, a very nice young lady, not pretty, but with an attractive air about her, but now, this morning, she looked quite plain, and her voice, usually so gentle, sounded quite different. Perhaps she wasn't feeling well, or starting a cold. Pleased with himself for having solved his little problem, he embarked on a fresh batch of verbs before their daily tour of the house. But now it was Olympia who named each object as they came to it, and today he promoted her to adding a suitable adjective as they started, as usual, in the sitting-room.

'A large chair,' said Olympia in her painstaking Dutch, 'a small table, a square carpet, some pretty flowers, a telephone . . .' She had come to the end of her adjectives and looked inquiringly at her teacher, who suggested the Dutch word for necessary. She repeated it obediently, thinking that as far as she was concerned it was nothing of the sort; it wasn't necessary for her to know about Waldo's girl-friends; she didn't want to know, all the same she was going to ask him the minute he set foot inside the house – she cared nothing for his private affairs, but she had a right to know. She came to a halt, these muddled thoughts racing round and round inside her head like mice on a wheel. 'I have a fearful headache,' she told the astonished Mijnheer Blom. 'I'm so sorry, you really must excuse me,' and fled from the room. Upstairs it was quiet with the peace of an old house. She sat on the bed in her room, and because she really couldn't help herself, had a nice cry.

She felt better presently, and when Elisabeth called some time later with the kindly purpose of escorting her to the shops, she was able to greet her quite naturally even though her face was still a little pale. She put on a coat and tied a scarf over her hair against the boisterous wind, snatched up her shopping list and joined Elisabeth on the short walk to the shops where she gave her order for the week's provisions, visited the butcher and the fishmonger and purchased a few household necessities, frequently corrected by the ever-helpful Elisabeth, who never seemed put out or bad-tempered. She was so kind, thought Olympia, struggling to make herself understood over the change, no wonder Waldo and Ria were so fond of her. They finished their shopping at length and walked on to collect Ria from school, and Olympia's mood was by no means improved at the sight of the little girl's obvious joy at seeing Elisabeth while she herself was greeted with remote politeness.

The rest of the day dragged until the doctor came home, and when he did, Ria was there, eating her supper in her pretty quilted dressing gown, while Olympia carried on a hesitant conversation with her; her Dutch was improving daily, but even so, without any help from the little girl, it was uphill work. All the same, she did her best and only paused when Waldo said from the door: 'You deserve a medal for perseverance, Olympia,' and whether he was referring to her struggle with his mother tongue or her efforts to break down Ria's hostility, she didn't know. He crossed the room and dropped a casual hand on her shoulder, then went to kiss Ria, and after that there was no chance to talk to him alone, not until Ria had been put to bed and she had come downstairs again to find him on the point of going to his study.

'There was a telephone call for you, from England,' she began without preamble, and was shattered to feel how she trembled inwardly; the trembling turned to stillness as she saw him halt and turn to look at her with suddenly alert eyes.

'England?' he questioned, and when she realized that he wasn't going to say any more than that, she went on:

'It was a woman, a girl I imagine, by her voice – it was pretty . . .' She swallowed the anger she had been nursing all day and went on steadily, 'She was anxious to speak to you – she didn't know who I was, but she told me not to tell your wife.'

He regarded her gravely, his face impassive. 'I take it she didn't give her name?'

'No. She said you knew the number,' and in the small silence which fell between them: 'Waldo, who is she?'

He answered her blandly, 'My dear Olympia, if you insist upon an answer, I will give you one, but I should very much prefer not to do so.'

'Never?' Her voice, to her annoyance, came out in an angry squeak.

The blandness had become silky. 'When the moment is right, I will tell you. Will that content you?'

It didn't, but she ignored that for the moment. 'Does it have to be so – so secret?' and greatly daring, because the bland face told her nothing: 'Do I . . . that is, does it concern me too?'

'Yes, it does.' She waited for him to say more than that, but apparently that answered both questions. Her temper nicely under control but spurring her on, she asked: 'Have you known her long?'

His eyebrows lifted. 'A few weeks – shortly after we were married.' Suddenly he smiled. 'I believe that we are at cross purposes – it is not at all what you think.'

She all but tossed her head. 'I'm not in the least interested in your private affairs,' she told him with immense dignity and utter mendacity, and felt annoyed when he answered calmly: 'In which case, this whole conversation has been rather a waste of time. Now if you will excuse me, I must make a telephone call.'

'Oh, certainly,' said Olympia pettishly. 'I'm sorry I've been wasting your time.' She added savagely, 'I have a great deal of knitting to do,' which absurd remark he acknowledged with a gentle nod and good-humoured agreement. She seethed as she watched his broad back disappear into his study and then suddenly her anger went, for what was the use of it? It was the kind of situation one read about in novels and the Sunday papers – someone in love with someone who loved someone else, only they always ended neatly in divorce. She shivered, quite unable to contemplate such a thing happening to her. But it could – Waldo couldn't be blamed if he had met someone he loved; he had made no bones about the terms of their marriage; no harm would be done if they were to part and he would be generous to her, although she knew that she could never take a penny of his money. She had hardly made herself indispensable, had she? Looked at from every angle, she was quite superfluous in his life. She picked up her knitting, attacking it with a ruthlessness which had no regard to the intricate pattern.

CHAPTER SIX

THAT same night Ria fell ill. There had been no warning, she had been peacefully asleep when Olympia peeped in on her as she herself went to bed. It was one o'clock in the morning when Olympia was awakened by a faint sound from the little girl's room directly above hers. She got out of bed, put on her dressing gown and slippers and ran upstairs. Ria was being sick, her small face greenish white, and when Olympia took a small wrist in her own steady one, it was to feel a racing pulse and a feverish warmth. She cleaned the child up gently, put on a fresh nightie, covered her carefully and ran downstairs to Waldo's room. He wasn't there, but downstairs the light in the hall was still burning and when she tapped on the study door and went in, he was there, sitting at his desk. Even then, with her mind full of Ria, she could see how tired he looked, his brows drawn together in a weary frown, but as he got to his feet his face became its usual placid self once more, although his eyes were alert.

'Ria,' she said, not giving him a chance to say anything, 'she's been dreadfully sick, her pulse is up too and she's feverish.'

He had come round the desk to stand by her and spoke with reassuring promptness. 'Let's go up and have a look at her,' and smiled so kindly at her that she choked a little. 'I had a look at her before I went to bed, she was fast asleep then.'

They were mounting the stairs together, his arm round her shoulders, for all the world as though they hadn't disagreed so sharply that very evening. 'Measles?' he mused out loud. 'There's plenty of it about – but she's been immunized. Something she ate? Supper?' He turned a questioning look on Olympia.

'A mug of cocoa, Marmite sandwiches, one sweet biscuit and an apple,' she answered promptly.

'Not supper, then. Appendix? Could be – we'll soon know.'

Ria had fallen into an uneasy sleep, but she wakened as they went in and was sick again. Waldo stood at the foot of the bed while Olympia cleaned up once more and then went to sit on its edge. He was quick and gentle, listened patiently to Ria's tearful little voice as he poked and prodded, and when he answered her his own voice was reassuringly quiet and calm. When he had finished he glanced at Olympia.

'Appendix – I'm pretty sure of it. We'll get her round to the hospital. Wrap her up warm – dressing gown and blankets will do – I'll go and telephone Piet de Haan, he'll have a look and see what's to be done.'

He said something jokingly to the little girl and went away, leaving Olympia to roll her carefully in blankets and collect a few things to take with her. There was nothing to put them in, though, so she flew down to her own room to fetch a small case of her own and when she got back found Emma on the landing. There was no time to explain in her slow Dutch, so she pushed a chair by Ria's bed and waved Emma into it and then ran downstairs again, this time to fling on some clothes and bundle up her hair. She was back again a few minutes before Waldo, who cast a glance at her sweater and slacks and tied-back hair and said with approval: 'Ah, good girl – I hoped you would come,' then turned to speak to Emma before picking up Ria.

He had found time to bring the car round to the door; they were away within seconds with Olympia in the back seat, Ria on her lap. The little girl was very quiet now, whimpering a little from time to time, clinging to her. The hospital wasn't far and Waldo took a short cut through the narrow cobbled streets. Even so, they were waiting for them, met at the door by a nurse and a porter with a trolley and a young houseman too. They went in swift procession to the children's ward, and they were expected there too, with a small bed turned down, Night Sister standing by it and a thin man with a stoop and thinning hair talking to her. Olympia was introduced rapidly before Waldo took him aside while Ria was put to bed. Someone took Olympia into Sister's office then, and gave her a cup of coffee and murmured kindly – conventional phrases of sympathy and optimism in excellent English; then Waldo was with her again, drinking coffee too and telling her cheerfully that it was an appendix and that she was to go straight to theatre where Piet would whip it out for her. 'She'll be back within the hour,' he told her, 'and home again in a week.'

'She's so little,' said Olympia.

He put down his cup and took her hand in a comforting grip.

'You're fond of her, aren't you?' he observed, 'despite the difficulties. I warned you that she would be a handful, didn't I, but I didn't expect her to fight against you.' He paused, looking at her from half closed eyes. 'And you have done a great deal for her, I have seen . . . It can't be easy for you, Olympia. I have sometimes wondered . . .' he paused and Olympia's heart stood still. Their quarrel was still fresh in her mind. What was he trying to say? Was he going to ask her if she would like to be free again? Before he could speak she said quickly, 'I don't know why Ria doesn't like me. Once or twice I've thought that she was beginning to like me just a little, and then – it's as if someone had warned her against me . . .' her voice trailed away and she knew that she had failed in her effort to make him understand for he took his hand away and said bracingly: 'That doesn't sound like you, Olympia. You must be feeling tired and a little overwrought. Would you like to go home? I can get someone to take you – Ria will be quite all right; I'll go into theatre with Piet and then stay until she's round.'

'I'd rather stay too, if you don't mind, I'll not be silly. And Waldo, I'm sorry about this evening; I had no right to speak to you as I did, it isn't as if I'm – we're . . .' She was bogged down in a sentence which she didn't know how to finish. 'We're friends; you said so, and I wasn't very friendly.'

She looked round as the door opened and Night Sister put her head round and said briskly: 'They're ready in theatre, Doctor.' She went away again, and Waldo got to his feet. It was just as though he hadn't heard Olympia's apology, for all he said was: 'You'll be all right here? We shan't be long.'

They were less than forty minutes, and within another half hour Ria had opened her eyes, declared that she was sleepy and closed them again. Olympia looked at the small, colourless face on the pillow, trying to see something of Waldo in it. There was nothing, but that didn't really matter; she was Waldo's child and because of that she loved her too. She bent to kiss the dark hair, then went to thank Piet de Haan, who was gulping down great draughts of coffee while he wrote up the chart. He was a nice man; she knew that instinctively, and when she thanked him he smiled with real friendliness.

'Waldo and I are very old friends,' he told her. 'Many is the night he has got out of his bed to see to my eldest – an asthmatic, you know; now I've had the chance to pay back something of what I owe him.'

She had gone home with Waldo after that and found Emma and Joanna waiting for them with more coffee and a great many anxious questions. It was half past four before they were all back in their beds.

When she got to the hospital after breakfast, driven there by Waldo on his way to the surgery, it was to find Ria sitting in a chair, looking washed out but perfectly happy. The doctor cast a knowledgeable eye over her chart, made a few inquiries, kissed her rapidly and with affection and went on his way, leaving Olympia, who had had the foresight to bring the little girl's favourite doll, Ton, with her. She also supplied news of Niko, a little hampered by having to use the same words over and over again. But her efforts pleased Ria, who gabbled away happily and when she got up to go, kissed her with something approaching affection so that Olympia walked back home with her spirits soaring at every step.

Life wasn't too bad, after all; Waldo had seemed glad to have her with him when they had gone to the hospital, although she had to admit that apologizing to him had been a waste of breath; perhaps he hadn't heard; he must have been worried about Ria despite his calm manner, and on this bright morning with the sun shining, even the awful shadow of the girl in London seemed vague and unimportant. She would redouble her efforts to make Waldo love her, although she hadn't the least idea how best to set about it, but at least she would try. Optimism came flooding back, bringing with it a gaiety which made Mijnheer Blom, when he arrived, reverse his opinion of the previous day; the young lady was pretty after all.

He had just gone when Elisabeth arrived and when Olympia told her about Ria's sudden removal to hospital, she was surprised to see her friend frown. 'What's the matter?' she asked anxiously. 'You look quite cross.'

Elisabeth smiled her gentle smile. 'Not that, Olympia, a little puzzled that I, an old friend and one who has loved Ria since she was a baby, wasn't told at once. I could have comforted her – gone with her to the hospital.'

'But it was one o'clock in the morning,' protested Olympia, puzzled, 'and we looked after her very well, you know, and went with her and stayed until she was back in bed again. I've just been there this morning with Waldo, she's sitting out in a chair, looking marvellous.'

Elisabeth said gently: 'You nurses – always so bright – I expect that you get hardened to illness and pain.'

'No, we don't. In fact I think we hate it more than people who don't understand it very well, only we mustn't show it; we're taught to hide our feelings.'

Her companion's lovely blue eyes studied hers. 'Do you? Do you really? Are you able to hide your feelings completely?'

'I imagine so.' She was still puzzled, Elisabeth was so intense, and usually she was such a serene person. She tucked her hand under her arm. 'Come and have some coffee and then come to the shops with me. I want to buy some wool.'

'More knitting? But Ria has two new pullovers and now you are knitting a cardigan.'

'This won't be for Ria. I thought I'd make Waldo a very thick sweater, ready for next winter. There's such a lot of him, it will take me the whole summer to knit it.'

She laughed as she spoke, but Elisabeth remained serious. 'But it will be a waste of time. He dislikes all sweaters but the cashmere ones he buys in London. I know because I always knitted them for him until he told me that he liked only these which he bought.'

Olympia poured her coffee. 'Oh, well, I'll start one for me – I like to have something to do, you know.' She was disappointed, but she wasn't going to let it show, and later that day, on her way back from the hospital, despite what Elisabeth had told her, she bought a vast amount of wool and a pattern. It was in Dutch and she would have to puzzle it out for herself, although Mijnheer Blom might help, or Emma and Joanna. She didn't think she would ask Elisabeth.

The house seemed very quiet without Ria, and now, if he had wanted to there was time enough for Waldo to talk to her when he got home each evening, but it seemed that he had had second thoughts about it, for after half an hour with her, talking lightly about nothing in particular, he went away to his study as he always had done, leaving her to wrestle with the pullover. But she had managed to make one small change; she had begged Waldo to let her sort his post for him every day. 'I can read quite well now,' she assured him not quite truthfully – 'not your letters, of course,' she added hastily, 'I won't open those.' She had looked at him as she had said that and gone a bright pink at the faint mocking smile on his face. 'Perhaps it's not such a good idea after all,' she had muttered, and was surprised when he said smoothly: 'On the contrary, it is a very good one. By all means do it, it will be a great help to me.'

So now she had the excuse of asking him about various small items in the post each day, so that sometimes he stayed just a little longer, but not often, and never, she felt sadly, of his own wish. But she had the bit between the teeth now with two visits to the hairdresser each week and something different to wear every day and a quite reckless extravagance in perfumes. It wasn't until the evening before Ria was to come home that he came back from his study with Niko at his heels to find her on the floor with her knitting spread out around her, poring over the pattern. She made a pretty picture in her red corduroy shirtwaister with her beautifully dressed hair, frowning a little in an effort to understand what she was reading.

She looked up as he came in and then down at the pattern again, because he looked so large and assured standing there smiling at her, that she longed to run into his arms – and that wouldn't do at all.

'Need some help?' His voice was casual.

'Well, yes – you see, it's a knitting pattern and I can't quite understand it.'

'If it's knitting, I don't suppose I shall either, but I'll have a look.' He got down beside her and read the instructions, a hand on her shoulder, his face very close to hers. When he had solved it for her he asked: 'For whom is this marathon knitwear, dear girl?'

'Well, I thought I'd make you a pullover for the winter, you know, but Elisabeth said that you only wore cashmere ones from London and it would be a waste of time, and I expect it is, only I wanted to.' She added breathlessly: 'You've given me so much – whatever happens, I'll never forget that, nor be able to thank you enough.'

She found herself on her feet, his hands at her waist. 'What a dear kind girl you are, and Elisabeth is quite mistaken; I always wear a thick sweater in the winter when I go into the country. I should like to have it very much, it will be something to remember for years.'

She spoke to his chin. 'The next line goes: "To remember with tears" – it's a bit from a poem by William Allingham.'

'The dreary fellow!' He kissed her suddenly and fiercely and then let her go. 'There, there's something you can remember without tears, I hope.'

He grinned at her and went back to his study and at dinner, half an hour later, he appeared to have forgotten that he had ever kissed her. A passing whim, she told herself and entered enthusiastically into his plans for Ria's return. But perhaps he hadn't forgotten after all, for later that evening as she was on the point of going to bed, he had wished her good night and added, 'You look sweet, and you smell sweet, Olympia,' he touched her hair lightly, 'and this – this is charming. You have changed in these last few weeks.' He laughed suddenly. 'Or is it I who have changed? And now you are knitting me a sweater.'

Olympia almost held her breath – had she been so obvious in her efforts to capture his attention? She said woodenly: 'It was only an idea – I mean, I can turn it into something else.'

'Don't do that – I promise you that I shall wear it.'

When she was in bed, she went over the conversation, word for word. What had he meant by changing? And had he meant for the better? And he had admitted that he had changed too. Had he been hinting about the girl in London, but in that case why had he told her that she looked sweet? To soften the blow, as between friends? She closed her eyes, half asleep; perhaps she had imagined the girl in London.

But she hadn't. Up early the following morning because she had several things to do before Ria came home, she went down to the sitting-room, still in her dressing gown and slippers; she had forgotten to fetch the new dress she had made for Ton the doll; it was in her work table in the sitting-room, and if she didn't get it now, it might get forgotten. She would take it up to Ria's room and put it by her bed, where it might be seen when the little girl got home.

The house was quiet, and because Niko would still be asleep in his basket in the kitchen she was extra careful to creep soundlessly down the stairs and across the hall. She was almost at the sitting-room door when she saw that the study door was open and that Waldo was there; she could hear his voice. He was on the telephone and his voice was low and clear. After the first few words she stood still as a mouse, shamelessly eavesdropping, for he had said with soft urgency: 'Don't telephone here any more, the risk is too great.' And presently he went on: 'I'll ring you, and when you write, send your letters to the surgery. My wife sorts my post and I don't want her to discover anything at this stage.' There was a pause and Olympia imagined the pretty voice in his ear. There was a hard lump in her chest, rising into her throat and threatening to choke her. She swallowed it back and waited for his next words.

'Send the bills to me,' his deep voice sounded un-hurried, 'and get whatever else you want at Harrods – I've an account there.' There was another pause, during which Olympia's imagination ran riot, but she checked it to hear him say: 'I'll come over within the next few days, we shall need to go to the solicitor once more, I imagine.' He was silent then until, apparently in answer to a question, he said quietly: 'I've no idea, but be there waiting for me. Good-bye.'

Olympia fled back upstairs as silently as she had come, the entire conversation dancing before her in letters of fire, his voice still in her ears. Her own fault for listening, she told herself bitterly, but who but a saint would have walked away after those first few words?

She walked straight through her bedroom and into the bathroom, where she ran a bath and lay in its warmth, fighting to keep calm. After a little while she dressed and did her hair with extra care, her face too, remembering as she did so how in the old days she had swept her brown locks into a severe bun and used only a minimum of make-up because she never had the money to buy it, and now her dressing table held a truly splendid collection of pots and jars, all of which she had bought, using them assiduously in the un-spoken hope that their contents would turn her into a beauty. They hadn't quite achieved this, but at least they had done a great deal for her, although nothing at the moment could disguise her miserable white face completely. She tried out one or two smiles, rubbed her cheeks to give them colour, and went downstairs to breakfast.

Waldo wasn't down yet, or perhaps he was already out with Niko. Almost guiltily she sorted through the post, arranged it in the piles she liked and retired to her own chair to read a letter from Aunt Betsy. It was a cheerful missive, full of a miscellany of news written with a dry humour and in a beautiful copperplate hand. Olympia found herself chuckling over it and when Waldo came in a few minutes later, she was able to greet him quite naturally. It was easy after that, for he had his letters to read and what conversation there was concerned Ria.

'I'll be back here at ten-thirty,' he warned her. 'Could you be ready by then? I'll fit in as many visits as I can after we have brought her home, but I may be late for lunch.'

Olympia was ready and waiting as the Daimler nosed its way into Balans and stopped to pick her up. Everything had been done; Ria's favourite lunch was in the course of preparation, Niko, neatly collared and wriggling on the end of his lead, was beside her, Ria's room, gay with flowers, was ready and Ton's new dress was on its miniature coathanger by the bed. She got into the car beside Waldo knowing that so far, at least, the day, on the surface at least, was going according to plan. If she was a little silent, her companion didn't appear to notice it and the journey was a short one. They went into the hospital together and up to the ward where Ria was waiting for them, and Olympia, in her best Dutch, thanked the nurses and Sister and handed over the small gifts she had brought with her. She talked to the houseman too, a nice young man who made her feel very much at her ease; she left him quite reluctantly when they finally went; he had made her feel attractive and worth talking to and she had needed that reassurance badly. Waldo, save for the one or two unexpected moments when he had actually seemed interested in her as a young woman and not as a faceless friend who ran his house for him, had remained remote even though he was as kind and placid as he always had been. Twice on their short journey to the hospital it had been on the tip of her tongue to tell him that she had overheard his conversation that morning and beg him to explain, even if that meant hearing about the girl in London – anything rather than his reserved friendliness, but she hadn't had quite enough courage.

She got into the back of the car with Ria and Niko, and having quietened her youthful companions, remarked, for something to say: 'That was all very successful, wasn't it?'

He glanced at her over one massive shoulder. 'Very – but did you have to be quite so forthcoming with young Willem?'

She answered him with an attempt at lightness, covering her astonishment as best she could. 'The houseman? But he was so friendly – I liked him.'

'That was obvious, but there was no need to show it so openly.'

He was driving through the busy morning streets and he didn't turn round, but from the glimpse she had of his profile she could see that he was angry. But then so was she; she had done nothing to justify his remark; laughed a little and talked a little with a pleasant young man of her own age who had made her feel good. Temper rose in a splendid wave within and a fine selection of angry retorts scalded her tongue, but she held them in check; it was Ria's homecoming and nothing must spoil that. She said in the mildest voice imaginable: 'If you want to tick me off, perhaps you'll do it later on.'

He didn't answer her, but when they arrived at the house, stalked inside with Ria, leaving her to follow with Niko. And Elisabeth was waiting for them; a surprise Olympia wasn't sure she was pleased about or not. It did mean, of course, that there would be less need for Waldo to maintain a friendly front in front of Ria; it also meant that Ria would get far too tired and excited. But Elisabeth was charming and very understanding. She sat quietly on the sofa beside Ria, holding her hand, and when they had had coffee and the little girl had calmed down a little and Waldo was on the point of leaving, she produced a prettily wrapped package, remarking in her soft voice that she hadn't known what to bring Ria and the moment the little girl had opened it she would go – perhaps Waldo would give her a lift as far as the Markt?

The ribbons of the gay little package were untied and the contents lifted out – a doll's dress, exquisitely made, an exact replica of the one Olympia had fashioned with such care, only this one put hers completely in the shade; there was a matching hat too and a tiny handbag and even a jacket. Olympia, asked to admire it by a delighted Ria, did so with commendable enthusiasm. It was of course pure coincidence that Elisabeth should have made something so exactly like hers, for how could she have seen it? Olympia had kept the little garment safe in her work-table all the time – well, perhaps not all the time, but even if Elisabeth had seen it she would never have played such a sly trick; the very idea was laughable, it was one of those quirks of fate. She saw the two of them off and then, on some excuse or other, ran up to the child's room and took the doll's dress on its absurd little hanger and stuffed it into the top drawer of the great painted commode on the landing outside her bedroom. She could get rid of it later.

It was during lunch that Ria asked her in a polite, hurt little voice why she hadn't given her a present too, and Waldo had looked up sharply as though he had suddenly been struck by the same thought, but he made no remark beyond chiding the little girl gently and then plunging into an account of Niko's behaviour while she had been away, so that there was no need for Olympia to reply. And what could she have said? she asked herself miserably, staring down at her plate, willing herself not to burst into childish tears. She was beyond the explaining she would have to do in Dutch for a start. It would sound like an excuse and if she produced it now, Ria – and Waldo too, for all she knew – would probably think she was merely copying Elisabeth in an inferior way. Her temper, never far from the surface since Waldo's unfortunate remarks that morning, rose again; a strong desire to throw something at him replaced her wretchedness. Her eye roved the table; there was a heavy cut glass decanter within reach – or the soufflé dish with the remainder of its delicious contents still sticking to it. Her hand itched to pick it up ... Waldo's voice, sounding surprised, brought her to her senses.

'Olympia?' it held faint inquiry, 'is something the matter?'

A silly remark and she longed to tell him so. Had he forgotten his nasty remarks already? She had not. She contented herself by saying:

'The root of the matter is in me. That's from the Psalms, I believe. Should I take Ria up to rest? If Niko goes with her, I think she will be quite happy and perhaps go to sleep.'

He carried the child upstairs and left Olympia to attend to her small wants, tuck Ton, resplendent in her new outfit, in beside her, and lift Niko on to the foot of the bed. 'I'll be back in a few minutes,' she said cheerfully in her halting Dutch, 'to see if you are asleep,' and was disconcerted at the look Ria gave her as she bent to kiss her. It was disappointment and a kind of resignation. She waved from the door and puzzled about it as she went downstairs.

On the landing below Waldo was standing with the top drawer of the commode open and in his hand was the doll's dress. He said nothing, but looked at her inquiringly, the ridiculous garment held carefully in one large, well-tended hand.

'If you must know,' said Olympia crossly, 'I made it for Ria – for her doll – but Elisabeth had made exactly the same one and so much better – and all the other things with it – the hat and the dear little jacket, even a handbag . . .' She gulped, frowned fiercely at him and stalked to the stairs and ran down them, and because she wanted to get away from him, rushed into the kitchen, shutting the door behind her with a decided snap. It was a disappointment that he made no effort to come after her; she heard the front door close within minutes, and when he returned, at teatime in honour of Ria's return, he was his usual placid self. They played cards after tea, just for half an hour, a noisy game of Happy Families, before Ria was borne away, quite willingly, to bed.

It would look foolish if Olympia were to knit the sweater when they were so out of tune with each other. She dressed carefully in a soft blue jersey dress, went downstairs and established herself in the small chair by the fire, for it was a cool evening. The room looked beautiful with its lamps casting a soft glow on the gleaming furniture, and the logs spluttering cheerfully in the hearth, but Waldo wasn't there. She picked up *Vogue* and began to leaf through it, but the models looked impossibly thin in their gorgeous clothes, almost ill; she had been thin like that, now she was becoming positively plump. Perhaps, she thought idly, she should go on a diet. Before their marriage she would have asked Waldo's advice and he would have laughed about it and she would have laughed with him. Thinking about it, Waldo hadn't laughed a great deal just lately.

He came in presently, but not before his secretary had telephoned from the surgery to ask where she could find him, and when Olympia, anxious to be helpful, said that she would give him a message the moment he came in, she had been asked to tell the doctor that there had been an urgent telephone call from London, and would he ring back as soon as possible.

She gave him the message as soon as he got in, in a wooden little voice which defied him to say anything at all; she wasn't surprised when he came back presently to tell her that he would have to go to London on the following day but hoped to be home again within two days.

CHAPTER SEVEN

As a small, lonely girl she had learned to hide unhappiness deep in her mind and fill the rest of it with matter-of-fact thoughts. She said now in a sensible voice: 'I'll pack a bag for you. Will you take the car?'

He stared at her as though he hadn't expected her to say that. 'No, at least, only as far as Schiphol, I can leave it there and pick it up on my return. I'll be away at the most for two nights. I can take morning surgery before I go and Wim and Paul must manage between them until I get back.'

He crossed the room to stand in front of her chair. 'Olympia, do you want to know why I am going to London?'

She kept her eyes on the fashionable model staring at her so disdainfully from the magazine cover. Did the elegant creature have problems too? she wondered. 'But you don't want to tell me,' she reminded him.

'No, I don't, but my reasons for not doing so are purely selfish and possibly a little foolish – nevertheless, if you insist . . .'

'But I don't.' She heard her voice, nice and cool and calm, but she didn't dare to look at him. 'Elisabeth is coming to dinner – her mother is away for the night and she sounded lonely.' She heard the small impatient sound and asked quickly: 'You don't mind?'

'No, why should I mind? She is like one of the family.' His voice had a strange note in it, and on an impulse she asked: 'Were you ever in love with her?'

He sounded utterly astonished. 'With Elisabeth? Good lord, no!'

But Elisabeth had been in love with him, probably still was. Olympia was all at once certain of that and wondered now why she hadn't known it sooner. Poor Elisabeth, unselfishly helping her in every way, giving advice, being her friend, cushioning her against the small awkward happenings which cropped up from time to time. True, sometimes the advice and corrections had been given when there had been other people to listen, and she had felt a fool, but Elisabeth hadn't realized that.

Her thoughts coloured by her friend's kindness, she welcomed her even more warmly than usual, and when Elisabeth embarked upon advice concerning the spring-cleaning, listened humbly, trying to remember all that she was saying. Only when she had gone, with Waldo escorting her to her car, did Olympia have a sudden uprush of rebellion; to spring-clean in the house was nonsense, it was always spotless under Emma's and Joanna's daily attention. Besides, the routine cleaning of curtains and carpets and the enormous chandelier in the sitting-room and the smaller one in the dining-room was undertaken at regular intervals. There would be no spring-cleaning, Olympia decided.

Curious to know Emma's opinion of her decision, she went along to the kitchen and made herself understood on the subject, only to have Emma overcome with surprise. 'But the doctor would be most annoyed,' she explained in the slow Dutch she used when she spoke to Olympia. 'We have not spring-cleaned for years; each week a room is turned out thoroughly, and that is done all the year round. Juffrouw de Val is mistaken.' She frowned. 'She knows as well as I do that the doctor dislikes it very much.'

Olympia ate a biscuit from a plateful on the kitchen table and said carefully: 'Perhaps I didn't understand.'

'But Juffrouw de Val speaks English to you, *mevrouw.*'

Olympia agreed that yes, she did, and ate another biscuit, praised Emma's baking, wished her good night and went back to the sitting-room. Waldo was there, standing by the window, looking out into the dark garden. He turned round as she went in, remarking: 'What a good friend Elisabeth is. She must have been of great help to you.'

Olympia agreed. She must reserve judgment; undoubtedly she couldn't have been listening properly to Elizabeth, or the kind soul had forgotten that Waldo disliked having his home turned inside out. Anyway, it didn't really matter. She made a few prosaic remarks about his journey, declared her intention of going up to bed after she had paid a final visit to Ria's room, and wished him a serene good night. No one, watching her going with calm leisure up the stairs, would have guessed at her unhappiness.

She saw him off the next day with a smiling face and no sign of the curiosity which consumed her. There had been little time to talk during breakfast and what they had said had been to do with Ria, and when he returned to pick up his overnight bag after surgery, she took care to keep the conversation vague and pleasant, never once mentioning his stay in London. And he hadn't wanted it otherwise, or so it seemed. Only when he was on the point of leaving he had held her close for a moment, and she, betrayed into lifting her face for his kiss, received none, only he muttered something in his own language as he touched her cheek with a gentle finger. He had left then, without another word, and she had remained in the empty hall, listening to the Lamborghini's purr dying into nothingness. A nice cry would have done her a power of good, but Ria was in the sitting-room, a little tearful because her papa had gone away, and although Olympia felt herself to be a poor substitute, at least she might be able to fill the gap until he returned.

And indeed she did. Elisabeth, whom Olympia had expected to visit them, didn't come; the two of them spent the day happily enough with Niko to divert them, the doll's house to set in order, and after tea, a rousing game of Happy Families, with Emma and Joanna roped in to make it more exciting. Ria had mastered the names easily enough, but Emma's efforts to pronounce Mr. Bun the Baker kept her laughing happily until bedtime, and while she was eating her supper, the doctor telephoned.

Olympia, who had had a hopeful ear stretched for the last hour or so, forced herself not to hurry to answer it, while her imagination painted a vivid picture of Waldo sipping champagne in the beautiful girl's flat, being diverted by her scintillating conversation and remembering impatiently that he really should telephone his wife . . . This absurd vision was so real to her that she positively snapped 'Hullo' in the crossest of voices and was brought back to reality immediately by Waldo's quiet: 'Hullo, Olympia, why are you upset?'

She made haste to deny this and added brightly: 'I hope you had a good trip. We've had a nice day, Ria and I.' She beckoned to the little girl, lifted her on to her lap and went on before he could speak, 'Here is Ria

125

to talk to you.'

Ria had a lot to say and took some time to say it. When at length she had finished, she gave the receiver back to Olympia and stayed where she was, in the crook of her arm. 'Hullo,' said Olympia once again.

'I'll be home tomorrow evening,' said Waldo in her ear. 'Anything from Wim or Paul?'

'No – Paul telephoned to ask if we were all right, he said they were coping very well.'

In the little silence which followed she clearly heard the tinkle of glasses and someone laugh – a woman. 'Must go,' she spoke stiffly in an effort to sound natural. 'Ria . . .'

'Yes, of course. Good night, dear girl.'

Her reply was glacial.

The next day dragged. Ria had made the swift recovery all healthy children make, and now, almost well again, wished to do all the things she shouldn't. Olympia devoted her whole day to her save for her Dutch lesson in the morning. Somehow she couldn't bear to miss that, it had become important to her that she should conquer the tongue-twisting language at the soonest possible moment. An ambition which Mijnheer Blom found most laudable and certainly possible; he had never had a pupil who worked so hard, he assured her, listening to her rendering of the conditional tense with a perseverance which did her – and him – credit.

Waldo had told Ria that he would be home in time to carry her up to bed, a nightly practice the moppet set great store by, and for once Olympia had no trouble in getting her bathed and dressing-gowned and downstairs in the small sitting-room, where her supper was waiting for her.

'It will please Papa very much if you have eaten everything up by the time he arrives,' counselled Olympia, and while the child ate obediently began, haltingly, to read *The Tale of Benjamin Bunny* in Dutch. It was pure chance that Elisabeth should call only ten minutes before Waldo arrived home, and pure chance that the first thing he should see as he entered the room was Elisabeth sitting on the floor beside Ria, with her arm around her. Olympia, who had taken the supper tray back to the kitchen and so had missed the sound of his arrival, got back in time to see Elisabeth spring to her feet and go towards him. She had almost reached him when he saw Olympia, and with the briefest of smiles for Elisabeth, went to meet her. He bent his head and brushed her cheek lightly and said: 'Hullo – you're wearing that pretty dress again. How is Ria?' and before she could reply, 'I've brought a guest with me.'

It was preposterous for her to imagine, even for one moment, that he had brought the girl back with him, but she did. She turned a stricken face to his, so that he caught her hand and exclaimed: 'My dear, what is it? You're tired – but Aunt Betsy won't need entertaining, you know.'

'Aunt Betsy?' echoed Olympia foolishly, and smiled brilliantly at him. 'Oh, dear – I'm so sorry, I thought . . .' She was unable to tell him what she had thought, and a good thing too, she realized later, because Ria came bouncing out of the sitting room and Waldo turned away to swing her up into his arms and then go to the door where Aunt Betsy was standing.

Olympia hurried forward too. 'Aunt Betsy, how lovely!' she cried, 'and do forgive us for leaving you to stand there.'

'Nonsense, my dear,' said Mrs. van der Graaf comfortably, 'husbands should have a few minutes in which to greet their wives. I had no intention of coming, I do assure you, but Waldo persuaded me to spend a couple of days here and I very much wanted to see you again – and Ria.' She turned to greet the little girl and then listened attentively to her dramatic tale, told with a gusto which set them all laughing.

'Well, come in,' begged Olympia at last. 'You'd like a drink, I'm sure – Elisabeth, you too.'

But Elisabeth declined in her pleasant, quiet voice; she would not intrude upon the family circle, she told them, a little wistfully, she had only called round to see how her darling Ria was getting on. Olympia went with her to the door and wished her her usual warm good night and asked her to come again while Aunt Betsy was staying. Elisabeth got into her car, saying vaguely that she had several things to do and perhaps she wouldn't have time.

'Oh, well, never mind,' said Olympia cheerfully. 'Come round when you like, you know you're welcome.'

Elisabeth smiled at her. 'I think that Ria begins to like you more than she likes me,' she commented lightly.

'She's very fond of you, but it would be marvellous if she would accept me as her mother. I – I'm very fond of her too, you know. I've thought during these last few days that she had begun to like me a little.'

The other girl nodded. 'Yes, I have noticed it also. Now I must not keep you, Olympia. Good-bye.'

Olympia went back indoors and forgot all about Elisabeth. Waldo might be in love with a dozen girls, but just for the blessed moment he was here, sitting in his chair, a look of complete contentment on his handsome face. Not because he was with her again – she knew that – but he loved his home and she ran it exactly as he wished and that made him happy. Besides, he had Ria again, sitting on his knee, undoing the gaily wrapped box he had brought for her. There was a glass at his elbow and Aunt Betsy, looking more elegant and unapproachable than ever, was sitting in a high-backed chair, sipping appreciatively.

'Don't get up,' cried Olympia as Waldo began to lift Ria from his knee. 'I'll get myself something.' She glanced at their stately guest. 'Aunt Betsy, what are you having?'

'Madeira, child, and an excellent one. How Waldo can drink whisky when there are wines like this, I cannot understand.'

He laughed. 'It does me good at the end of a day. Olympia, try some of the Madeira, I brought some back with me.'

Ria had her present open at last – there was a doll inside the box, a pretty baby doll, wrapped in a shawl. 'No clothes!' shrilled the child, investigating.

'Look in the package underneath,' advised the doctor patiently.

There were balls of knitting wool, lovely pale colours and knitting needles besides. 'Mama knits beautifully,' he pointed out, 'nice woolly things, just right for a baby, and I daresay she will teach you how to knit too.'

'Ton will mind,' objected Ria.

'No, she won't, she will be very glad to have a baby to play with. You have had Ton for three years, she's a big girl now, almost as big as you.'

Olympia had listened to this conversation and understood most of it. Waldo was repairing the fiasco of the dress she had made for Ton; even if he didn't love her, he was so kind . . . She said in her slow Dutch:

'Now, that is a splendid idea, and there's plenty of wool to make Ton a jumper. We'll start tomorrow, shall we?' She finished her drink. 'What about bed, poppet?'

Ria was borne upstairs, kissed good night by the doctor and left to Olympia's gentle care. Only as she was preparing to leave the room, with Niko frisking along beside her, the new doll tucked up with Ton beside the little girl, and the bell just nicely within reach in case anything was needed, and the night light on the chest of drawers, did the child ask: 'May Tante Betsy come and see me?'

Olympia bent to kiss the small forehead and tried not to notice Ria's quick turn of the head to avoid it – and only an hour or so ago she had thought that the moppet was beginning to like her . . . she said quietly: 'Of course, darling, I'll ask her.'

Aunt Betsy got to her feet at once and surged from the room. 'And I will go to my bedroom – the one I always have, I expect? and tidy myself,' she told them, and chuckled cosily. 'That will give you ten minutes to yourselves, won't it?'

'The kitchen – Emma!' exclaimed Olympia, suddenly breathless at the idea of being left alone with Waldo, and made for the door.

'Olympia.' The doctor's voice was placid, but it halted her. She asked: 'Yes, Waldo?' a little too brightly, only half turning round, the very picture of a hindered and harassed housewife, and he said on a half laugh, 'I'm sure that Emma can cope with whatever emergency there is in the kitchen.' He got up and strolled over to her. 'Why did you look like that, dear girl?'

'Like what?'

'Like someone whose heaven had fallen. Who were you expecting, Olympia?'

She gave him a wild glance. 'No one – I mean, I was surprised. I didn't expect Aunt Betsy.'

His voice was bland. 'Ah, yes – of course. By the way, I've changed the car.'

'Changed the car? The Lamborghini?' She forgot she was anxious to get away from him, she even took a couple of steps forward.

'Yes. Now that I am a married man, it isn't very suitable, don't you agree? Tearing around on my own isn't quite the same thing as driving my wife and daughter.'

She stared at him, trying to fit the girl in London into this new happening; perhaps he had given the Lamborghini to her – she would be able to go down to Dover and meet him and they would tear off anywhere they wanted to go . . . She blinked at the wild strength of her imagination, at her rage at the thought of him loving anyone else, even though he had never loved her. She schooled her voice to mild inquiry. 'Oh? What sort of car?'

'A Rolls-Royce – a Corniche Convertible. I had someone looking out for one for a week or two and he had the incredible luck to find a man who had just taken delivery of one and then had second thoughts. Come outside and have a look.'

It was a wonderful car, a gleaming gunmetal grey, perfection itself. Olympia, quite overcome, peered and poked and then got inside to try its super comfort, longing to ask the wifely question as to whether he could afford it. She was quite startled when he said, 'Don't worry, my dear, I'm rich enough to indulge my tastes and, I hope, please you.'

'Oh, you have,' she assured him. 'It's super – I liked the Lamborghini, but this one is just right for you, somehow.'

He smiled a little, leaning against the door. 'Should I be flattered?'

For a moment she had forgotten the girl in London and Elisabeth and Ria not liking her. 'Yes, I think you should,' she told him shyly, and then, afraid that she might say more than she ever meant him to know, she got out of the car and added sedately: 'Ria is going to love it.' She turned her back on him and asked carefully: 'What's happened to the Lamborghini?'

He swung her round to face him, his hands on her waist. It was quiet and there was no one about; it seemed a long time before he answered her. 'She's gone to someone who will appreciate her,' he told her. 'Let's go in and rescue Aunt Betsy.'

Mrs. van der Graaf was a delightful guest; she reappeared at exactly the right time, just before dinner, made light conversation while they drank their sherry and had just the right amount to say for herself at the dinner table. She ate delicately but with pleasure, praising the ratatouille, the salmon steaks with herb butter, accompanied by broccoli and a French dressing and tiny new potatoes, and the splendid apple pie which Olympia had made that afternoon. They went back to the sitting-room for their coffee and Aunt Betsy, sitting erect, as always, gave it her opinion that Olympia was an excellent housewife. 'A delightful meal, my dear,' she beamed. 'Waldo must be very proud of you.' She glanced across at her nephew. 'You must give a dinner party and let everyone see what a treasure you have captured, dear boy.'

He smiled back at her. 'Indeed we must, it will give Olympia an opportunity to air her Dutch, too. She is making great progress.'

They talked light-heartedly until bedtime. A delightful evening, thought Olympia, on the way upstairs to bed with Aunt Betsy, and as she thought it, had it shattered by the ringing of the telephone in Waldo's study. He was still in the hall. Olympia, looking back, saw his quick frown as he went to answer it; she heard, too, his quick: 'Yes? I'm home – wait a minute . . .' He had closed the door then and she, with barely a pause, went on up the stairs beside her guest, talking rapidly about nothing at all in an effort to appear totally unaware of Waldo's words.

It was while they were having their coffee the next morning, with Ria happily engrossed in her doll's house on the floor between them, that Olympia remarked to her guest: 'I asked Elisabeth to come in while you were here, but she wasn't sure if she could manage it – I expect you know her very well.'

Aunt Betsy stirred her coffee and added a thought more sugar. 'Very well indeed,' she said in a dry voice. 'She has been a great help to you, so Waldo tells me.'

'Oh, yes. I don't know what I should have done without her. She explained how Waldo liked things and told me when I made mistakes – and I made dozens – still do.'

'I am sure that you would have managed very well even without her help, and you had Waldo to go to for advice.'

Olympia had no idea how stricken her face looked.

'He's very busy,' she pointed out defensively. 'I couldn't go running to him each time I wanted to know something.' She had her eyes on her cup and didn't see her companion's bright glance. 'I was terrified of letting him down – it's quite true what Elisabeth says, you know, I'm not used to this kind of life.' She looked up at last. 'You know, Aunt Betsy, I really didn't think that Waldo was rich – really rich. I've had to get used to that.'

'And if he lost all his money tomorrow, would you have to get used to that too?'

Olympia laughed. 'Yes, of course, but it wouldn't matter at all.'

Aunt Betsy clicked her tongue. 'A pity you weren't able to come with him to London, but of course you had to stay with the little one. You get on well with her?'

There was no point in prevarication with Aunt Betsy; she would keep on, like a bulldozer, until she got what she wanted.

'No. I've tried very hard and once or twice I thought that she was beginning to like me. She's always very polite and her manners are beautiful, it's as though she's been told not to like me, but that's absurd, of course. She loves Elisabeth – understandably. I think,' she went on, mentally damning the consequences, 'it would have been far better if Waldo had married Elisabeth.'

'Ah,' said Aunt Betsy profoundly. 'Far better for everyone, my dear?'

'Everyone.'

'You are, of course, mistaken, but it is not for me to enlighten you. Why do you suppose Waldo married you?'

'He wanted someone to run his home and look after – mother – Ria. He knew that I was unhappy with Aunt Maria and he thought it a good idea if – if we married, so that I could do these things for him and get away from Aunt Maria.' She shot a defiant look at Mrs. van der Graaf. 'And please don't tell me anything different.'

'Why should I when what you tell me is quite true, my dear?' queried her guest, dashing down any half-formed hopes Olympia was cherishing. She went on in a chatty way: 'Of course Waldo has known Elisabeth for a great many years, before he married you. He depended upon her when it came to household matters and looking after Ria. She is an old and trusted friend, but no more than that.'

'She must have been a great help after Estelle died.'

'Indeed she was, quite indispensable.'

Olympia thought that she detected dryness in her companion's voice once more. 'Elisabeth is a marvellous friend,' she declared warmly, 'and so gentle and self-effacing. She could have hated me, you know, and made life quite unbearable.'

Aunt Betsy agreed to this in a non-committal manner and asked: 'And do you go out much? Waldo has so many friends – and have you visited Amsterdam and The Hague? Arnhem is a delightful place, too, and not so very far away.'

Olympia poured more coffee, gave Ria another biscuit and took time to answer. 'Well, Waldo is very busy; he works most evenings. We went to dinner at Wim's house and I met Paul and their wives. And we all went to Zierikzee – Waldo has a friend living there with an English wife, she's very nice. They have a lovely old house . . .' She became aware that she was babbling and stopped. There were surely other occasions she could tell Aunt Betsy of, but that later gave her no time to think: 'And Waldo has not taken you out excepting on these occasions?'

'I've been quite happy – I like just being here, and I've heaps to do.'

'What do you do, Olympia?' asked Aunt Betsy inextricably.

Olympia hadn't expected this cross-examination; she said feverishly: 'Oh, I talk to Emma about the meals and do the flowers, and of course I have a Dutch lesson every morning, and I go to the shops, and of course there's Ria.'

Her companion made an impatient sound. 'You are in fact being a good housewife.'

Olympia raised troubled eyes to the older lady. 'I've tried, but I'm not sure that I've been successful.' She choked back a wish to tell Aunt Betsy everything – Waldo's impenetrable, reserved friendliness, and all the mistakes she had made, and the time and money she had spent on her hair and her clothes and the care with which she dressed each day in the hope that he would notice, and last but not least, her awful suspicion about the girl in London. Instead she said in a bright voice: 'I really should take Niko out for his walk. Would you mind very much if I left you with Ria for a little while?'

Aunt Betsy didn't mind in the least; going out of the house a few minutes later, Olympia could hear her in lively conversation with her small great-niece. They sounded very happy together. She attached Niko to his lead and followed his chubby, gavotting little figure out of the front door and did a brisk circuit of the Abbey, entering its large courtyard by the further gateway, and so home, her mind busy with an idea which had just entered it. Ria wouldn't be able to go to nursery school for a week or two, so would it not be a splendid idea if someone – Mijnheer Blom, perhaps – should give her a few lessons each morning? She would soon get restless once the novelty of the new doll had worn off and the doll's house palled and the brighter days were coming; she would want to go out playing with her small friends or going for long walks with her and Niko, and she wasn't quite strong enough yet. Mijnheer Blom could give her some lessons to do and perhaps she could sit in the same room while she herself had her Dutch lesson, and it might be a sound footing upon which to build a new relationship between them. She would ask Waldo.

There was no chance to speak to him alone during lunch, and he was called away directly after it, but that evening, after Ria was in bed and the two ladies were gossiping over the outfit they were knitting for the new doll, there was opportunity enough, for Waldo, instead of going to his study as he usually did, remained with them, reading his paper and joining in their conversation from time to time, but before Olympia saw a chance to mention her plan, Aunt Betsy declared her intention of going to bed and she was barely out of the door before Waldo declared that he had work to do. Just as though, thought Olympia sadly, he couldn't bear to be alone with her, and yet before they married they had spent a lot of time together and he had appeared to have enjoyed her company, but of course, if he had met someone else ... She tried not to think about that as she said in a cool voice:

'If you could spare a moment, Waldo, there is some-

137

thing I would like to talk to you about.'

She had her eyes on her knitting, and didn't see the sudden sharp look he gave her, although his voice was calm enough. 'Of course, what is it?'

'Well, I wondered if it would be a good idea if Ria were to have just a few lessons each day – perhaps Mijnheer Blom would teach her for half an hour and then give her some work to do while he gives me my Dutch lessons. You see, once she has got over the excitement of coming home and the new doll she's going to be bored; she's full of energy, and no child of that age would sit still all day unless she's given a jolly good reason – she loves school, doesn't she, and this would be the next best thing, just for a week or two.'

He said thoughtfully: 'That might be a good idea, Olympia. I'll speak to Blom.' He added: 'That's clever of you, dear girl.'

She was quick to take his meaning. 'You agree that it might help us to be friends – having lessons together? I thought that too, and it's something I want above everything else – I'd do anything.'

He was leaning against the door, his hands in his pockets. 'Yes, I know that. Another matter – I wondered if we might invite Wim and Paul and the girls over for dinner one evening while Aunt Betsy is here? Elisabeth too.' He smiled slowly. 'It will give you a chance to show off your cooking as well as your Dutch.'

She agreed pleasantly and wondered if he would have thought of it if Aunt Betsy hadn't suggested it first. 'Which day?'

'Sunday evening? That would be the simplest for me; I'm on call and it's easier to be home. Will you see about inviting everyone?'

She said that yes, she would and went on to wish him good night.

'You haven't forgotten that I'm going to Utrecht in the morning? If I'm back in time, how about a run in the car during the afternoon? Aunt Betsy might like that.'

Olympia started to pack up her knitting, turned out the lamp on the table beside her, and got to her feet. 'I imagine she will be delighted. You might take Ria with you.'

His eyebrows rose. 'But of course you will come with us too.'

She swept past him, her colour becomingly high. 'No, I will not!' she snapped. 'Just because we have a guest staying and you feel like entertaining her, places you under no obligation to do the same for me.' She hurried across the hall and actually had a foot on the bottom stair when she was caught, turned round and held firmly.

'Now, now,' said the doctor at his most placid, and then: 'You know, you should lose your temper more often, it's highly becoming.' He kissed her lightly. 'Now go to bed and don't be a silly girl.'

He spoke with a bland good nature which hurt almost as much as his impersonal kiss had done. It was just as well, she thought later, that he couldn't see her now, crying with helpless rage as she got ready for bed.

She went down to breakfast early, piled the doctor's post tidily, sat the dressing-gowned Ria in her chair, then took her own place at the table and began to write out a menu for the coming dinner party, but she didn't get far with it, indeed she wasn't giving it her whole attention; she was listening for Waldo's steps in the hall as he came back from his walk with Niko.

He wished her a cheerful good morning, good-naturedly allowed himself to be half smothered by Ria's embrace, and sat down to his breakfast. Aunt Betsy, declaring that she had reached the age when she might indulge herself in small whims, took hers in bed, so that the meal was dispatched with a minimum of talk, the doctor muttering from time to time over his letters and Ria piping up with some childish observation. Olympia poured her husband's coffee, set the toast rack ready to his hand, buttered bread and added a wafer of cheese for Ria, and crumbled toast on her own plate as she drank her coffee. She looked up presently to find Waldo looking at her over a sheaf of papers.

'You're not eating,' he observed pleasantly. 'Do you feel all right?'

'Yes, thank you.'

'Then have some toast, dear girl, we don't want you to lose any of those very attractive pounds.' He passed her the toast and she obediently took some as he went on: 'I'll lunch in hospital and be back about two o'clock.' He got up, preparing to go. 'We will go to Veere – it's a delightful place and only a few kilometres away. We can have tea there and drive back through Domburg. I'm afraid I must be back for evening surgery, though.'

'I think,' said Olympia, addressing his shirt front, 'that I may not have the time to come with you . . . the dinner party, you know.'

'In that case we'll cancel the dinner party.' His voice was bland, and when she peeped at him it was to find him smiling at her so that her heart lurched around her chest like a thing gone demented.

'I'll come,' she told him.

He came round the table, dropped a kiss on Ria's dark head before she felt his hand on her shoulder. 'Spoken like a true friend, my Olympia.' The hand was gone, too quickly. With a brief good-bye he was gone.

They had a delightful afternoon. Veere, in the spring sunshine, looking like a mellow watercolour painting from the Golden Age. They parked the car and strolled round the tiny place, then climbed the stone staircase in the Campveerse Toren Hotel, to sit at a table in the window and drink their tea. The window overlooked the harbour and the cobbled street beside it, lined with beautiful old houses. Waldo pointed to one of them. 'A friend of mine lives there – a doctor,' he observed. 'Marius van Beek – haven't seen him for years. He married an English girl, a charming little thing called Tabitha. Paul told me that they were in England for a few weeks, otherwise we could have called to see them. I'll bring you over again when they're back.'

'What is Tabitha like?' asked Olympia.

'Small, quiet, one of those faces which isn't pretty until you get to know it well. She's just had another baby, that makes a boy and a girl.'

'That makes two English girls living quite near.'

'There are others, too, I believe – I hear of them from time to time, but until now I've never bothered, but I'll find out more about them if you like.'

'A splendid idea,' pronounced Aunt Betsy in her cosy voice. 'Besides the pleasure it will give Olympia, it will be splendid for Ria; she will make new friends. It doesn't do for a child to grow up lonely.'

She looked at them in turn, her blue eyes limpid, and

the silence shouted at them until the doctor said smoothly: 'You're probably right, Aunt. And now if we have finished, how about taking a quick look at Domburg?'

The rest of the day was agreeable enough; the doctor, his little party safe home again, went away to his surgery. Ria was bathed, given her supper and whisked away to bed, leaving the two ladies to retire to their rooms to tidy themselves for dinner and then meet downstairs, where they sat knitting like two Furies and talked gentle nothings until Waldo came home again. And after dinner, since he declared that he had no work to do, he kept them company over the coffee cups and presently suggested a game of Scrabble, played in Dutch, of course, so that Olympia's knowledge of that language might be further improved.

She worried a good deal over the dinner they were to give; true, she knew the guests well enough to make light of anything which might go wrong, but like any young wife, she was anxious not to let her husband down. She spent a good deal of time closeted with Emma, worried as to what she should wear and booked an extra appointment with her hairdresser. Aunt Betsy was leaving them on the day following the dinner party; she had friends coming to stay with her, she said, and added in her cosy way that young married people should be left to themselves and she for one had no intention of playing gooseberry for more than a few days. 'Not that I have needed to,' she finished rather tartly, so that Olympia blushed and Waldo looked first surprised and then amused.

They all went to church on Sunday morning, a custom which Olympia was beginning to enjoy, partly because she sat next to Waldo during the lengthy sermon, and partly because the hymns were sung so slowly that she had a splendid opportunity to practise her Dutch, singing them. Aunt Betsy, regal in grey wool and mink, marched along with Ria holding her hand, leaving Olympia and Waldo to walk together. It was a chance to tell him how successful Ria's lessons were proving. 'Mijnheer Blom is such a nice man,' she said warmly, 'and Ria likes him – besides, it makes her feel very important, drawing her letters and counting beads while I sit close by having lessons too.'

The doctor agreed rather absently. 'That's a pretty hat,' was all he said, and before she could show surprise at this remark: 'We don't seem to see much of Elisabeth just lately.' His voice held a faint query.

'She said she had a lot to do – she didn't say what, she's coming this evening, though. Do you want to see her specially?'

She heard his chuckle. 'No – no more than one always likes to see old friends. And if you meant are we going to retire into a corner with a bundle of legal papers, no, we aren't.'

She felt awkward, because that was just what she had been thinking. Which made her deny it all the more hotly. 'She depends on you quite a lot, I expect, for advice and so on.'

'And do you depend on me, Olympia?'

The church bells pealed out, almost drowning her voice. It was necessary to be truthful and she stopped so that she might look at him. 'I try not to,' she told him seriously. 'It wouldn't do, would it?'

'Why not?' His voice was very quiet.

'Well . . .' She paused; the bell had stopped – they would be late. 'You know why as well as I do.' She started to walk on. 'We shall be late.'

He didn't answer, but presently, sitting squeezed rather tightly beside him because Aunt Betsy was sharing their pew as well as Ria, she was uncomfortably aware that he looked at her from time to time, long thoughtful stares and quite unsmiling. The impulse to slip her hand into his was so sharp that she clenched her gloved hands together on her lap, so that they shouldn't escape.

They walked back as they had gone, with Aunt Betsy sailing majestically ahead with Ria, deep in conversation. But Olympia and Waldo were silent; they had walked half-way across the Abbey courtyard before Waldo slowed his pace. 'Olympia,' he began in the bland voice which she recognized as inflexible, 'you didn't answer my question.'

But she didn't have to; Joanna came hurrying to meet them, spoke urgently to the doctor and hurried away again. 'Mevrouw Ros,' said Waldo, 'has chosen this moment to go into labour – I'm afraid that I must leave you, dear girl. Let us catch up with Aunt Betsy and then I will go on ahead – and do not wait lunch for me; Mevrouw Ros, as I should know after aiding her on four happy occasions, is not to be hurried.'

He strode off, leaving the three of them to make a more leisurely progress while Olympia, limp with relief at not having to answer his questions, wondered what she would have told him if Joanna had not arrived at such an opportune moment.

He didn't come home until they were having tea, and after she had made sure that he had all he needed for his comfort, she excused herself and repaired to the kitchen to make sure that everything was going just as it should. She had chosen the meal with care; a paté made to Emma's own recipe for starters, turbot for the main course, boiled delicately, decorated with lobster coral and cucumber, and served with a rich and creamy lobster sauce, new potatoes and a green salad on the side, with a sprinkling of red peppers to make a splash of colour, and for afters she had fallen back on apple pie once more because everyone seemed to like it. She had made it of ample size with a mouth-watering crust, and there was cream, served in the William and Mary silver cream jugs, which together with the rest of the table silver, used as a matter of course by the doctor, were a never-ending source of delight and pride to her.

She had decided on an amber-coloured jersey dress in a simple style which set off her slender shape to great advantage and made a splendid background for the coral brooch, and when she was dressed a glimpse in the mirror assured her that her efforts had been worth while. She wasn't a vain girl, but she would have been blind not to see the difference in her appearance since she had married Waldo. She nodded her head with pleased satisfaction, sprayed herself discreetly with Madame Rochas and went along to see if Ria was asleep before she went downstairs to wait for her guests.

There was still half an hour before they could be expected to arrive; she inspected the table a little anxiously, found it perfect, and went into the sitting-room. There was no one there, but the bright fire in its wide hearth and the soft glow of the lamps welcomed her in the early dusk. She wandered round restlessly, picking things up and putting them down again until Waldo's step in the hall sent her flying to sit in a chair, ready to greet him with cool composure despite her racing pulse. He came in unhurriedly, very elegant in his dark grey suit, and stood looking down at her. 'That's charming,' he remarked. 'I like the colour.' His look became thoughtful. 'Stay where you are,' he begged her. 'I shan't be a moment.'

She had no time to wonder what he was about; he was back within a moment or so, a long leather case in his hand which he gave to her.

'I should like you to have these,' he told her. 'They were my mother's –indeed, all the van der Graaf wives have worn them for many generations. They should go well with that dress.'

She opened the box under his eye. There was a coral necklace inside – a three-stranded rope of vivid pink, fastened by a round clasp of coral and pearls set in an intricate gold filigree. There was a bracelet too, a solid gold band set with cabuchon corals with pearls between.

Olympia touched them lightly with her fingertips and asked: 'For me? You mean that you are giving them to me?'

He was leaning over the back of his chair, staring at her. 'Yes – are you not a van der Graaf wife?'

'Yes, but you have given me so much.'

He answered her in astonishment. 'I? But I have given you nothing.'

She began painstakingly to list his gifts. 'My engagement ring and the brooch,' she touched it with a hand as she spoke, 'and that Dior scarf I liked and all my clothes and that funny china angel and my suede handbag, and . . .'

He held up a large hand in mock horror. 'Stop, I beg of you! I had forgotten the half of them – such trifles. Come here and I will fasten the necklace for you.

'And now the bracelet,' he advised, and turned her

round to face him. 'The necklace is charming, but the bracelet is perhaps a little heavy for your wrist – you are so small, I must find something daintier.'

'Oh, no,' she declared, 'I like this very much, I've never had any jewellery . . .' She stopped; it was unfair to arouse his pity and she would despise herself for it, too. 'Thank you very much, Waldo.'

He didn't let go of her wrist but took her other hand in his too and she waited, her heart pounding fit to crack her eardrums.

'Olympia . . .' He stopped as the door opened and Aunt Betsy came in.

The others came then, with Elisabeth last, apologizing for being a few minutes late. She crossed the room to meet Olympia half-way and kissed her and then said in her clear, soft voice: 'How very nice you look, Olympia, and you are wearing the van der Graaf corals – I thought that Waldo was never going to give them to you, although you deserve them above anyone. It must have been so difficult for you, learning our way of life, and this big house and having servants – and then Ria, such a naughty little girl not to like you.'

She stopped suddenly, her hand over her mouth. 'Oh, dear – I shouldn't have said that, and everyone listening.' She looked round the room with a contrite face. 'Please forgive me.'

There was a nasty little silence before Olympia, with a slightly heightened colour, said reassuringly: 'There's no need to be sorry, Elisabeth. Everyone here knows I'm – I'm new to the job and I could never have managed if you hadn't helped me, and you still do help me. I'm glad you like the corals, they do go very well with this dress, don't they?'

She was aware that Waldo had come to stand beside

her; she felt his hand, very light, on her waist. He said good-naturedly: 'I think Olympia deserves diamonds at the very least. I must start saving up.'

There was a general laugh at this little joke and Elisabeth was given a drink and swept into the light chatter which her ill-timed observations had interrupted. But for Olympia, chattering away gaily to her guests, the evening had been spoilt; she felt sorry for Elisabeth and each time she glanced at her she felt sorrier; she looked as though she was ready to burst into tears at any moment, although it was plain that she was making a great effort to behave normally, and after dinner, she slipped into a chair close to Waldo, watching his face; as though she were trying to draw reassurance from his very placidity.

But if anyone else noticed anything amiss, they gave no sign, the dinner had been eaten, praised generously and Olympia, becomingly pink-cheeked, had ushered her guests back into the sitting-room where over coffee the conversation, thanks to Waldo's skilful guidance, became lighthearted and amusing and remained so until everyone got up to go; all but Elisabeth; she stayed where she was while Olympia and Waldo saw their guests away, wished, in turn, Aunt Betsy a good night, and returned to the sitting-room.

Elisabeth almost ran to meet them. She flung herself into the doctor's arms and now she made no attempt to stop her tears. 'Oh, Waldo,' she sobbed, 'I have been so thoughtless, all those things I said – I was not thinking you understand? They were private things which only we know about – I shamed poor Olympia and I am so upset. Your aunt looked as though she wished to kill me, and the others stared so.'

He patted her shoulders and said something in

Dutch which Olympia, standing forgotten, couldn't catch, but she heard him well enough when he said: 'I'll take Elisabeth home, she is upset – and she was always a sensitive girl.'

And I, thought Olympia silently and in sudden rage, am insensitive and not in the least upset, I suppose. Elisabeth had been unwittingly unkind at her expense, but she didn't hold it against her; even the best of friends could drop a clanger at times, but someone – Waldo, for instance – might take the trouble to find out if she felt upset too; after all, she had been made to look pretty inadequate, to say the least. Her listeners must have got the general impression that before her marriage to Waldo she had been living on a very inferior social plane – and so, in all fairness, she had, but that was hardly the point. She answered now with forced cheerfulness, 'Yes, do,' kissed Elisabeth good night and shut the front door after them. But once they had gone her uplifted mood disintegrated into a snappishness which sent her off to bed; let Waldo find the house silent and no one about when he got back. Upon impulse she took off the necklace and the bracelet, laid them in their case and took it along to his room and laid it on the tallboy, then flounced back to her own room; let him have the things back again, for obviously she wasn't quite suitable to wear them, she told herself, flinging off her clothes in a very haphazard way, kicking her expensive shoes over the carpet and dragging on her dressing gown. She had been made to feel like a kitchen maid in front of her guests, she decided, her temper rising. She picked up her hairbrush and began to drag it through her hair, then stopped this self-torture because someone was tapping on the door.

Waldo – with the case in his hand and looking most satisfyingly annoyed. 'I gave you these, Olympia,' he told her in a quiet voice, 'they're yours now.'

'And I've given them back.' Her voice was a little loud; it also held a decided wobble because he really did look rather angry. 'I refuse to accept something which I quite obviously am not worthy of.'

'Of which I am not worthy,' he murmured. 'You're getting your grammar muddled.'

She shot him an infuriated glance. 'Grammar has nothing to do with it,' she snapped. 'I'm neither entitled nor deserving of the family corals.'

He put the case down on the bedside table and leaned against the door, his hands in his pockets, looking as though he were rather enjoying himself. 'Rubbish, you deserve them all right, and as my wife you are entitled to them.'

'Neither reason makes them acceptable to me,' she declared, 'and there was a third reason, wasn't there? They went well with my dress – well, I've decided I don't like it any more, so now I won't need the corals to go with it.'

He crossed the room so quickly that she jumped to her feet and retreated behind the stool she had been sitting on. Of no use, of course; he plucked it out of his way as though it had been a feather and gripped her shoulders. 'Vixen,' he said pleasantly, 'you surely haven't let poor Elisabeth's ill-chosen words upset you?'

'Since you ask – a little late in the day – yes, I have allowed them to upset me. To be reminded at my first dinner party that I'm not quite – quite,' she paused for a word, 'upper crust, is upsetting, nor did I like to be told in front of your friends that I had failed with Ria.

I daresay,' she went on bitterly, 'the child realizes that I come from a different background – children are sharp little things, you know. But don't,' she went on, her voice regrettably shrill, 'allow my feelings to disturb you – not that I suppose that to be likely. And now you will be kind enough to go away.'

To her surprise and secret dismay, he went.

CHAPTER EIGHT

OLYMPIA went down to breakfast the next morning a little uncertainly with Ria dancing along beside her. Waldo was still out with Niko, so she had time to see the post as usual. There was one envelope with a London postmark, the handwriting large and flowing and feminine. She itched to open it as she laid it on top of the pile, but whatever her own feelings that morning, Waldo, when he joined them, certainly didn't seem to share them; he wished her good morning in a perfectly normal voice, kissed Ria, tickled her to make her giggle, besought Niko to behave himself and sat down to his breakfast. Olympia, pouring coffee, watched his quick frown as he saw the letter, but he didn't open it at once, and when he did he read it with no change of expression, and presently he put it back in the envelope and gave his attention to his meal with the inquiry as to what time Aunt Betsy had decided to leave them, for all the world as though they were the best of friends, thought Olympia peevishly.

Aunt Betsy, she told him coldly, had decided to go back by plane, and hoped that he would get her a seat before he left for the surgery.

'I'll see what I can do – it shouldn't be too difficult at this time of year. Has she any preference as to time?' He had risen and reached for the telephone extension. 'If she goes on an afternoon flight I could run her over to Schiphol.'

'She said she didn't mind but she hoped you would be able to drive her there.'

He smiled as he put through a call. 'We'll all go, shall we?' He didn't look at her or wait for an answer but talked for a few minutes on the telephone before replacing the receiver. 'Three-fifteen – couldn't be better. Will you let her know?'

She nodded and got up to wipe Ria's face. She kept her back to him while she did it and was glad of it when he observed casually: 'I've been thinking, Olympia – it might be a good idea if you were to take driving lessons and have your own car, that will make you independent of me in the future.'

Paving the way for solitary years ahead? she wondered. Even if he didn't want her as his wife, he would take care of her, she knew that. It would have been wonderful if she could have been a combination of Elisabeth and the unknown girl in London, instantly loved by Ria and with Waldo at her feet. She stifled a giggle, for the idea of Waldo at anyone's feet was a little too much, even for her imagination, and made haste to murmur a suitable answer to his remark.

The morning passed rapidly with Aunt Betsy demanding everyone's attention in her pleasant, commanding way, and Ria, excited at the prospect of an outing, getting terribly in the way. They lunched without Waldo and by some miracle they were ready for him when he arrived shortly after the meal.

They were to go in the Rolls; Olympia got into the back beside Aunt Betsy while Ria, very cock-a-hoop, was perched beside the doctor. The child was quite well now, and longing to go back to school, a wish which had that very morning been vetoed with consequent tears, but now all that was forgotten; she sat beside Waldo, entertaining him with her childish chatter, while the two ladies carried on a conversation

153

which, on Olympia's part at least, was a trifle forced.

Aunt Betsy took a bit of getting off – she refused to be hurried for a start; her luggage, and there was a great deal of it, had to be checked, dealt with and consigned to official care; she required information on all and every aspect of her journey and expected to be accorded the care given to a V.I.P. To all these vagaries Waldo responded with good-humoured patience, while Ria and Olympia kept out of the way and did as they were told. Not that they minded that; neither of them had been to Schiphol before, it was a treat which they were both enjoying, and for the time being at least they were friends. But this was short-lived, alas, for once Aunt Betsy was safely airborne and the three of them were back in the car, speeding back to Middelburg, Ria's mood changed. She wanted to go to Elisabeth's house for tea, she informed her papa, and when this was quietly refused, threw a fit of tantrums which the doctor calmly ignored and Olympia seemed powerless to stop. It was a relief to get home and hurry the cross little girl indoors, while the doctor, with a murmured word of apology, drove himself to the surgery. By the time he got back again, Ria had exhausted herself, but not before declaring that she didn't like Olympia at all, that she wished she had never come to live with them, and that nothing would be nicer than that she should go away again. Olympia, quite puzzled at the child's outburst, preserved a calm front, but by the time Ria was in bed she was quite exhausted, and Waldo's cool assumption that she had had no difficulty in calming the child down hardly added to her good humour. They ate their dinner together in a slightly restrained atmosphere, and when Waldo, reverting to his old habit again now that their guest had gone, went to his study, she felt nothing but relief. She went to bed early and fell at once into an exhausted sleep which lasted until the early hours of the morning, which gave her plenty of time to lie awake thinking about the future.

Ria was unnaturally quiet during breakfast; she had apologized to Olympia at the doctor's calm instruction, but Olympia had seen the sullen set of the small mouth and the narrowed eyes; she was still very much disliked, despite the apology, but she accepted it cheerfully, and the morning, taken up with Mijnheer Blom, passed much as usual. It was after he had gone that Ria began to cry again and no cajoling on Olympia's part could discover the cause. It was a relief when Waldo came home for lunch, for Ria cheered up at the sight of him, regaled him with an account of her lessons, asked a great many questions about Aunt Betsy's journey and evinced so much interest in his replies that the meal passed off a great deal more happily than Olympia had dared to hope.

It was after lunch, when Ria was in the kitchen to attend to Niko's meal under Emma's eye, that the doctor asked, 'What is the matter, Olympia? Here is Ria full of false gaiety and you wrapped in gloom. Trouble between you again?'

'Yes, Waldo. I've tried hard to be friends, but she doesn't like me, and you can't blame her for that – why should she, after all? She's a dear little girl and very loving – it's I who am at fault, though I don't know why. I suppose she doesn't remember her mother? I mean photos of her and people talking about her, so that she seems real to her still?'

'I think not. Estelle died soon after she was born; she can have no possible recollection of her.'

'No. Perhaps she remembers you feeling sad, though.'

His eyebrows lifted. 'My dear girl, I didn't feel sad, not in the way I imagine you to mean. I didn't love Estelle.'

'Not love . . . but you love Ria?' she stuttered a little in surprise.

'Very much, but Ria is not my daughter.'

Her eyes widened and her mouth dropped open. 'Not your daughter?' she reiterated stupidly. 'I don't understand.'

'Probably not; you didn't know about it – how should you? It is something which no one knows.' His voice was cool. 'She is the daughter of my young brother and my wife. Willem was killed a week or so before they were to have been married.' His voice had become very calm, but she could see that his hands were clenched so that the knuckles shone white and his face was bleak. She saw something else too – out of the corner of her eye. The door had moved – had opened a fraction which widened very slowly as she watched. Someone was outside, listening. Please God, not Ria, she prayed silently and cried urgently: 'Don't say any more, Waldo, not now,' and watched the door imperceptibly close again.

The doctor spoke heavily. 'You're quite right, there is no reason for you to be told, is there? It's something I have done my best to forget, for Ria's sake.'

'Is that why you married Estelle?'

He had turned away to look out of the window.' Yes, and if by that you mean did I marry her because I was in love with her, no, I did not. We had very little liking for each other, but my brother's child had to have our name, it was the least I could do.'

He came back from the window and picked up his case and walked to the door. It seemed to Olympia, watching him unhappily, that he was always going away. The thought made her say in a strong voice: 'Waldo, that isn't what I meant at all. Please wait, there's something . . .'

He interrupted her, his voice kind, his face as placid as it always was. 'Shall we forget this?' he suggested. 'I know that I can trust you, Olympia, never to speak of it to Ria – or anyone else. It need never be spoken of again.'

He had gone before she could think of anything to say and she heard his voice, quite normal and cheerful, as he spoke to someone in the hall.

The door opened again, and just for a second she thought that he might have come back and she took a step forward without knowing it. But it wasn't Waldo, it was Elisabeth, her pretty face smiling. As she came in she said in her sweet voice: 'Hullo, Olympia – I met Waldo on the doorstep as I was on the point of knocking and he let me in. I've come to see if you would like to come shopping. I have a few small things to buy and I would enjoy your company.'

Olympia smiled at her. Dear Elisabeth, kind and thoughtful and prepared to like everyone, even if she did create awkward situations. An afternoon out would be pleasant, but she shook her head regretfully.

'I'd have loved it, but have you forgotten that I told you Mijnheer Blom is coming again this afternoon because he can't manage tomorrow morning? – he'll be here at any moment.'

She had hardly finished speaking when Ria came running in, and although her manners were too good to allow her to ignore Olympia entirely, she accorded her only the briefest glance before running to Elisabeth, whom she greeted with every sign of delight. At least there was one thing to be thankful for, thought Olympia, watching them chattering happily together, there was nothing in the little girl's face to indicate that she had been the listener at the door. Relief swept over her in a warm tide so that she asked quite gaily: 'Did Niko eat his dinner, Ria?'

The child nodded briefly and turned back to Elisabeth, asking her something in an urgent voice.

'Ria wants to come with me – may she do that? I shall not be long, you understand – half an hour, an hour. I will bring her back for her tea.'

Olympia glanced at Ria; the child wanted to go and there was no earthly reason why she shouldn't. She agreed readily enough and went upstairs with the child to brush her hair and help her put on the new red anorak they had chosen together only that week. That had been a shopping expedition too, although brief and certainly not successful. Ria had gone with her unwillingly and even when she had been invited to choose the colour she wanted, she had been remotely polite about it, there had been no fun, no giggles, only a well-brought-up little girl minding her manners. Olympia stifled regret, wished her a cheerful good-bye and watched her skip down the staircase to join Elisabeth waiting in the hall. They went out of the house together, hand in hand, leaving it quiet and empty. Olympia, with nothing much to do, picked up her knitting once more, but after a row or two she let it fall into her lap. Perhaps she would take a walk, a really long walk, with Niko, but she had to dismiss this idea immediately; Niko had already had a long walk, and a healthy bout of exercise in the garden besides; he was tired, indeed, he was stretched out before the cheerful little fire crackling on the hearth. She got up and wandered to the window, the fine spring day was deteriorating slowly; great grey clouds were nosing their way over the washed-out blue of the sky, presently it would rain.

She turned away from this sombre outlook in time to see the doctor walk in once more.

'Elisabeth gone?' he wanted to know idly.

'Yes, to do some shopping. Ria's gone with her.'

He went to the bookshelves and began to search for what he required. 'They're devoted to each other,' he observed, 'and Elisabeth knows how to handle her.'

Olympia had picked up her knitting again, now she cast it down in a muddled heap on the floor and got to her feet. Something inside her had snapped, freeing her so carefully squashed doubts and unhappiness; overriding her love.

'It is a great pity,' she observed in a clear voice, 'that you didn't marry Elisabeth. Even if you don't love her, she loves you, and it seems to me that it would have been absolutely super for all three of you.'

She started for the door, caught her knitting with a foot, kicked it viciously aside with disastrous results, and stalked past the silent doctor, shutting the door with emphasis behind her.

Perhaps if she had had the leisure to think about, she might have felt compelled to go back at once and apologize for her outburst, but Mijnheer Blom, arriving at that very moment for her extra lesson, made that impossible. She greeted him with quite insincere warmth and whisked him off to the small sitting room, where for the next hour or so she sat attentively throughout his painstaking lecture on Dutch grammar.

She heard not a word of it, and while she stared down at the rows of verbs he was explaining so carefully, she saw none of them, only Waldo's face. She would apologize; she had been spiteful about Elisabeth, who had shown her nothing but kindness since she had arrived in Middelburg and had never once given her cause to worry. Even if the poor girl was in love with Waldo, she behaved as an old friend and nothing else, and he – he had never given her cause to worry either – not with Elisabeth at any rate. She was ungrateful as well as spiteful, she told herself, her eyes fixed in grave attention on her teacher's face; he had given her so much, this man whom she had married.

She went to the door with Mijnheer Blom and saw him safely away and then crossed the hall to the sitting-room. Outside its door she paused, drew a deep breath and went in, the speech she had been rehearsing between bouts of verbs ready on her tongue. Only Waldo wasn't there, and when she inquired of Joanna, it was to discover that he had gone out and would probably not be back until after dinner.

Olympia, still in an uplifted mood, went to retrieve her knitting, and over a soothing cup of tea began the difficult task of disentangling it. She had expected Ria home by now, but probably Elisabeth had taken her back to have tea with her and would bring her presently. The knitting took a long time. She became so absorbed in it that by the time it was finally dealt with, she was shocked to see how late it was. Ria should have been back by now; it was almost her supper time. Olympia waited another uneasy half an hour, and then, rather worried, telephoned Elisabeth's home. But it wasn't Elisabeth who answered, but her mother. Her daughter wasn't there, she told her in some surprise;

she had taken Ria home at least two hours previously, had returned to collect her case and driven herself off to stay with friends in Belgium.

Olympia felt small icy fingers crawl up her spine; perhaps Mevrouw de Val hadn't understood her very well; she tried again. 'But wasn't Ria with her when she returned?' she asked carefully.

The voice at the other end of the wire sounded faintly impatient.

'Elisabeth brought Ria back here for tea and drove her home before returning here to pick up her things. I daresay Ria is hiding somewhere in the house – a joke – you know what children are.'

Olympia thanked her and rang off; possibly the little girl was hiding, it was the kind of prank that small children loved to get up to, but why hadn't Elisabeth come to see her? Or had she been in such a hurry that she hadn't waited but given Ria a message? She fought back a nasty feeling of panic. Of course the child was hiding somewhere, that was the only answer. She began to search the house, going from room to room, missing no possible spot where Ria might be. When she had finished the house, she tackled the garden, the garage and the little potting shed behind it. Then, just to be quite sure, she climbed the stairs once more, right to the top of the house, and went through the attics once again, this time with a fine tooth comb.

Back in the kitchen, she asked Emma and old Mevrouw Holst, who came in to clean the silver, if they had seen anything of the little girl, although she knew what their answer would be before she had spoken. She left them getting Ria's supper, fetched her coat and went out into the street. Here she drew a blank, as she did in the Abbey courtyard; all the same she searched thoroughly. It was dusk by now and she was becoming really frightened; Ria was such a little girl, easily frightened too, and quickly tired even though she had recovered from her operation. Olympia hurried back to the house to fetch a torch and make certain at the same time that Ria hadn't returned home. It was chilly as well as almost dark by now, but she had to search once more. If only she knew where Waldo was! She had telephoned the hospital, but they had no idea, nor had his secretary at the surgery; Olympia hurried downstairs, left careful instructions with Emma, and ran to the door.

Waldo let himself in as she reached it and put out a steadying hand to slow her down.

'In a hurry?' he asked coolly. 'Never running away?'

'No, I'm not – I'm going out to look for Ria, she hasn't come home. I've been out once – I thought she would be back at teatime . . .' the story came tumbling out, she had quite forgotten that they had parted on bad terms only a few hours earlier; all she knew was that here was Waldo, looking safe and solid and able to reduce everything to normality again. 'I've hunted high and low and I telephoned the hospital. Oh, Waldo, do you suppose something has happened to her?'

He had put his bag down on the console table, now he opened the door again. 'I have no idea,' he said bleakly. 'Stay here – I'll take the car.'

'Let me come with you,' begged Olympia, and was shocked to silence by his icy: 'Better not, I don't think you would be of much help. A pity you didn't do something about it sooner.'

She forgave him this unfair remark even while it hurt so bitterly – it was the kind of remark she would have made herself in like circumstances, even though it was so cruelly unjust. The door shut quietly behind him and she heard the car's powerful purr recede into the distance. Its last echo had barely died when she went out of the door herself. She had no idea where to go, but her feet took her automatically through the archway into the Abbey close. It appeared to be empty, but in the gathering gloom one couldn't be too sure. She walked round its perimeter, and satisfied that there was no small figure lurking in its shadows, walked on, out of the opposite gateway, more slowly now, peering on each side of the narrow cobbled lane as she went.

She crossed Lange Delft and turned into the Herenstraat, towards the canal. There were few people about; everyone would be indoors having their evening meal. Her way led her along Turf Kaai and towards the Vlissingen road and the light had almost gone. She thrust her hand into her pocket and touched her small torch, and her fingers closed around it thankfully. Clutching it like a talisman, she suddenly knew why her feet had led her this way, towards the main road; Ria had told her – she couldn't remember exactly when; she had been naughty – that one day she would ran away to England and live with Aunt Betsy, and when Olympia had inquired if she knew how to get to England she had replied that yes, she had only to go to Vlissingen and get on a boat. If the child had run away there was a good chance that she was carrying out her childish threat.

Olympia quickened her pace; the whys and wherefores she could think about later on, now it was vital to find Ria. She passed the row of small houses lining the main road; they were small and flat-faced with tiny front gardens, very neatly kept, and presently they gave way to solitary brick-built villas, each standing in its own small piece of ground, and then finally to allotments, dotted with small wooden sheds. Here she slowed down; if she were a very small girl, running away from home, those huts would represent cosy security to someone who had missed her supper and whose short legs would be tired after the long walk from home. Olympia turned in at the first open gate and began a laborious search, trying the door of each hut in turn and when she found one open, peering inside by the light of her torch. Probably she was trespassing, undoubtedly if someone saw her she would have a hard time explaining her actions, but she was past caring about such things by now.

She had made her way across half of the allotments when she noticed a shed standing a little back from the path, and its door was ajar. Ria was inside, curled up on a sack of potatoes and fast asleep, her small face tear-stained and grubby where she had wiped the tears away. Olympia's heart turned over with relief and pity at the sight of the forlorn little creature; she arranged the light of the torch so that its narrow beam shone away from them both and then got on the sack too, taking Ria gently in her arms as she did so, and talking gently the while, so that when the child woke she wouldn't be frightened. But Ria woke with no trace of fear and said at once, to break the hard core of tears in Olympia's breast, 'I'm so glad to see you, you came to find me like a mama would, didn't you?' She dug her head into Olympia's shoulder and submitted to some fierce hugging, while Olympia, almost speechless with relief and happiness, marshalled her Dutch. 'Papa is looking for you,' she managed. 'He is very unhappy.'

The small face, soggy from too much crying, stared at her through the almost dark. 'He is not my papa.'

Olympia caught her breath. 'Did he tell you that?'

Ria shook her head.

'Then who did, little one?'

'I'm hungry . . .'

'So am I, we'll have a huge supper presently. Who told you?'

'Elisabeth. This afternoon when we had done the shopping – when we were going home.' Ria began to cry again, and Olympia hushed her gently while she translated laboriously to herself. So it had been Elisabeth at the door – Elisabeth, the quiet, gentle family friend. She said slowly in ramshackle Dutch, 'Your papa loves you, Ria.' She got off the sack and took off her coat and wrapped the child in it. 'We're going home now – Papa will be so happy to see you again.' She kept her arms round the child. 'Is that why you ran away?' she asked, making her voice matter-of-fact.

'Elisabeth said I wasn't anyone's little girl, she said I had best leave home because now you were there no one would love me.' Ria drew a tearful breath.' She said that before you came with Papa.'

'That you must leave home because of me?' Olympia's Dutch was hopelessly mangled by now, but the child seemed to understand.

'No, not then. She said you wouldn't like me, so I wasn't to like you.' She leaned her small person against Olympia. 'I'm tired.'

'Then I shall carry you. Here we go – oops-a-daisy!'

Ria flung an arm round her neck and giggled sleepily. 'Oops-a-daisy,' she essayed, and giggled again, then burst into fresh tears. Olympia sat down again and held her close – a good cry would do the moppet good. It would do her good too, she thought wryly, but surely Waldo would be so overjoyed that his small daughter – no, not his daughter, but certainly as well loved as any daughter of his would be – had been found, that he would forgive and forget – they might even begin again ... She stifled her straying thoughts and said in English: 'There, there, darling, all better now.'

She was kissed damply. 'I'll be your little girl,' Ria told her between sniffs, 'if you will be my mama.' Even in half-understood Dutch this was wonderful news indeed. Lighter of heart than she had been for some time, Olympia picked up her small burden and began to make her careful way back to the road.

It wasn't a great distance back to Middelburg, a mile perhaps, and Ria was quite heavy, but she didn't notice the weight. She had gone almost a third of the way when she heard a car coming towards them. The Rolls; she knew the sound of its engine, a fine silky hum, rushing in their direction. She went to the side of the road and stood quite still, waiting for its powerful headlights to catch them in their beam. The car swept past, slowed, turned and purred powerfully back to them. It was quite dark by now; she couldn't see Waldo's face as he got out of the car, but she heard him saying something quick and fierce in his own language as he bent to take the now sleeping child from her arms. He said quietly: 'Get in, Olympia,' and she did as she was told, her joy at seeing him slowly congealing under the anger she could sense but not understand.

He settled Ria on to her knee and closed the car

door on her before going round and getting into his own seat. As the car slid forward he said in a tight voice: 'I told you to stay at home.'

So that was the cause of his anger. 'I know,' she spoke eagerly. 'I'm sorry, but after you had gone I remembered Ria telling me about going to England from Vlissingen, and I felt certain that's what she was doing – it was a lucky guess.'

She received no reply and after a minute, unable to keep it to herself any longer, she told him in a happy little voice:

'Ria's going to call me Mama, Waldo. Isn't it marvellous, and she says she'll be my little girl.'

Still silence. Quite deflated, she sat beside him, silent for the rest of the short journey. Perhaps he was too upset to speak; he must have been very shaken. She didn't know much about men and their feelings, she reminded herself. Come to that, she didn't know much about men – Waldo especially.

Emma was waiting for them in the hall as Waldo carried Ria in and straight upstairs to her room, where he laid her on her small bed and left Olympia and the housekeeper to undress her and tuck her up. She hardly wakened as she was undressed and given a warm drink, but when these small chores had been done and Olympia bent to kiss her, she opened her eyes and said sleepily, 'Now I will kiss you too,' and did so, wreathing her arms round her neck in a tight hug.

As Olympia straightened up she saw Waldo standing there, watching, and because he looked so remote, her smile was uncertain as she went away to her own room. He would want to talk to Ria, to wish her good night and tell her how glad he was to have her home again. She went downstairs half an hour later, her face and hair carefully done and wearing a blue pinafore dress with a paler blue blouse beneath it – Waldo had said once that he liked her in blue.

She found him in the sitting-room, writing at the small secretaire by one of the windows, but he got up as she went in, and she, still buoyed up by Ria's capitulation, didn't notice the sternness of his expression. She hurried across the room to him, exclaiming as she went:

'Oh, Waldo, I believe it's going to be all right, after all! Ria does like me, she may even begin to love me in a little while – like her own mother.' She came to a halt before him, her face alight with happiness. 'How lucky it was that I found her.'

'A triumph for you, Olympia,' his voice was silky, 'at the expense of a small child's fright and unhappiness, so that she felt forced to run away from her home, and all this so that you might play the heroine and rescue her, to find your way into her trusting little heart.'

He hadn't raised his voice at all, but its silkiness made her shiver. 'I believed that you loved her and I trusted you.'

'I – I don't understand,' she looked at him in bewilderment; surely he wasn't angry because she had found Ria.

The blue eyes which met hers were icy. 'No? Did you believe that no harm would be done if you told Ria that I was not her father – that she had no father or mother?'

She was speechless, and after a pause he went on slowly, 'I didn't believe Elisabeth, not at first . . .'

Elisabeth, that snake in the grass, thought Olympia, and all this while I've been taken in – we all have. She wanted Waldo and this was her way of turning him

168

against me. And he had believed her; reluctantly, but none the less, he had listened to that soft voice. She said suddenly in a firm voice, 'Please telephone Elisabeth and ask her to come here, now.'

The doctor's eyebrows lifted. 'My dear girl, you cannot hope to gull me into thinking that you didn't know that she was going to Antwerp.' His voice changed suddenly. 'Olympia, did you know?' And when she nodded, his eyes grew hard again. 'So that you knew her to be safely out of the way.'

She was making no impression at all. Her heart sank, but all the same she tried again. 'You believed her?'

'Not at first, I . . .' He paused and then went on in a smooth, cold voice. 'Eventually, I had no other choice. Elisabeth is an old friend, I have known her for many years . . .'

'And you don't know me at all . . .' She was trying to keep calm, but her voice had risen.

He ignored her interruption. 'Elisabeth is devoted to Ria, she would hardly invent such a cruel tale, nor would she cause the child any distress. How could you be so cruel, Olympia, to tell Ria something which she need never have known, and to break your word to me. Thank God Elisabeth was there to comfort the child, though she had no idea that Ria was so heartbroken and that she would run away from us all.'

Olympia choked back her rage; if she lost her temper now she might say the wrong thing. She could explain and Ria would bear her out, but she would have to wait until the morning. She would ask Ria who had told her and she would do it with Waldo there. All the same, she tried just once more. 'Look,' she said in a carefully controlled voice, 'please let me tell you . . .'

His 'No' was firm and determined. 'I don't want to

know, Olympia. Probably you did it for reasons of your own, but I don't wish to know them. And please give me your promise that you will say nothing – nothing to Ria, no questions, no hints, no breath of the whole miserable affair. I will talk to her tomorrow and explain all she needs to know, and then the entire matter is to be forgotten.'

She doubted if she would ever forget it, and even if Waldo did, it would remain between them for the rest of their lives and nothing she could do would destroy it, and now he had taken her chance of explaining from her. 'I promise,' she told him.

He nodded and then, true to his edict, asked her in a perfectly normal voice if she would care for a drink before dinner. The forgetting was to take place as from now. She swallowed an hysterical giggle and was horrified to discover that tears prevented her from speaking. She made short work of her sherry under his surprised eye, and muttering something about Emma and the kitchen, escaped.

The sherry went at once to her head. She climbed the stairs and sat on the top tread, one arm round the carved balustrade. She would have to think of something; sooner or later Elisabeth would come back and she could tax her with her conduct, but in the meantime she would have to pull herself together. Helped enormously by the sherry, she went to the kitchen where Emma gave her a surprised look and asked: 'Is anything the matter, Mevrouw? You look strange. I was just going to take in the soup.'

Olympia smiled and nodded and went back to the sitting-room to tell Waldo that dinner was ready. He put down his glass and stood looking at her. 'Olympia,' he said, and his voice was kind now, 'I hope that you will do nothing impulsive because of this – Ria must not be upset a second time.'

'You mean run away or something?' she asked bluntly, her voice a little loud by reason of the sherry. 'No, I won't do that – I won't run away, although that was probably what I was meant to do.'

He frowned. 'That sounds like a wild statement, what did you mean by it?'

'Nothing – just a wild statement. The soup will be getting cold.'

It was a rather silent meal. Nothing could be sillier, thought Olympia, nibbling her way through a meal she didn't want, than two people making conversation when they had nothing to say to each other. She stole a look at her husband; he wasn't eating much either, but his face wore its usual placid expression again – his dear face, she thought foolishly, and she would never be able to tell him that, he would be shocked and upset if she told him that she loved him to distraction. She had only to open her mouth and say so. He looked up and the words she longed to say turned themselves into an offer of more trifle. She wondered what he would say if she told him that Elisabeth had planned the whole thing; she must have been very quick about it, for she had had only a few minutes in which to decide how to turn Waldo's words to her advantage, and presumably she expected that Olympia would give in at last, and faced with Waldo's anger and Ria's dislike, go back to England. Well, she wasn't going to. She would be here, waiting, when Elisabeth came back. It wasn't until she was in bed, still thinking about it, that she remembered that Waldo wasn't in love with Elisabeth; he would never want her for his wife, she was certain of that. The girl in London, forgotten until that moment loomed into her mind to keep her sleepless for the greater part of the night.

It was obvious the next day that Ria had neither asked any questions nor volunteered any information about her escape. Waldo must have explained matters very satisfactorily, for she was quite happy and undisturbed, and to Olympia's delight, displayed an affection for her which she had never shown before. It was at the end of an endless day that Waldo came home to tell then that they were all going over to London to visit Aunt Betsy. 'I have one or two matters to attend to,' he explained, 'and a change will do us all good.'

Ria received the news with rapture, Olympia rather more guardedly.

'Do you really want me to come with you?' she asked.

'But of course, do you not wish to come? I thought we might go to one or two theatres.'

So he had meant what he said, he had forgotten; she had never believed that he would, or could; he had forgiven her too, even though he believed that she had done all the things of which he had accused her. She loved him very much for that. 'I should like to go very much,' she said quietly. 'How long shall we be away?'

His voice was coolly friendly. 'I can't say. It rather depends upon someone I must see while I am in London.'

For no reason at all Olympia remembered the girl. A wave of misery engulfed her. She had been a failure; at least, perhaps not quite, but she had hardly been a sparkling success, had she? Thinking about it, she knew now that she would have been more of a success if

Elisabeth hadn't pointed out her mistakes and short comings quite so often, but that didn't matter now. Waldo must bitterly regret marrying her; she caught sight of her reflection in the wall mirror and saw that she was hardly looking her best; she was wearing a sober grey dress which drained all the colour from her already colourless face and she hadn't bothered over-much with her hair. If I were a man, she told herself silently, I wouldn't look twice at you, let alone marry you, and she transferred her gaze to the doctor, poring over a map with Ria. It was a fine muddle they were in. She remembered that someone he had to meet in London; let him sort it out for himself, he would get no help from her. Rage bubbled up, devouring her carefully preserved serenity. For the hundredth time she wondered why he had married her; Elisabeth had been there, waiting for him to open his arms, and even though he hadn't wanted her, there was this sweet-voiced creature in London. Olympia snatched up her ill-used knitting. It wouldn't be fit to wear by the time she had finished with it, but what did that matter? It gave her something to do. She began on it now, appalled at the strength of her feelings; she had always thought that love would be gentle, and when necessary, self-sacrificing. It was nothing of the sort; it was over-whelming, a flame of feeling which brought out the very worst aspects of her character.

CHAPTER NINE

THEY were to go to England in a week's time and the intervening days were filled agreeably enough with shopping and the English lessons Ria had demanded; it seemed that she was bent on mastering the English language within a few days, and indeed, she was quick enough to learn all that Olympia was teaching her. As for the doctor, he was seldom at home. Taking a week's holiday would put extra pressure on his two partners, so that he felt compelled to do more than his share before he went. He was usually gone now before Olympia got down in the morning and if he came home for lunch it was a meal eaten in a hurry with no chance to talk. Nor did he join them for tea; it was as though he were making his work an excuse for avoiding her, and she, supposing this to be so, forced a cheerful face, devoted herself to Ria and in the slow evening hours before he came home at last, occupied herself at his desk, neatly entering appointments, answering the telephone and sorting his letters.

Two days before they were to leave Waldo came home unexpectedly early. Olympia was in the study, laboriously sorting circulars from the post, while Ria, dressing-gowned and ready for bed, sat before the small fire gobbling down her milk and biscuits which Olympia had just fetched from the kitchen. It was a splendid sign, she thought, watching the little girl with an amused smile, that Ria had developed such a good appetite. She had changed a good deal since Olympia had found her in the shed; she seemed content and very sure of the love they were both taking such pains to show her; certainly the happy little face she turned to the doctor as he came into the room was proof of that as she jumped to her feet to be hugged and kissed. He groaned in mock horror at the barrage of questions he was expected to answer as they laughed and talked together. But Olympia couldn't help but hear the change in his voice as he turned to speak to her. Answering his polite inquiries as to their day, she wondered if this was how it would always be now; this reserved politeness and deliberate avoidance of her company; if so, how would she ever learn to bear it? But her face as she turned to answer him was serene enough.

She left his letters neatly piled and said pleasantly: 'I'll go and see about dinner. Are you going out again? Would you like it earlier?'

He had got down on the rug beside Ria and Niko had joined them. They made a charming domestic picture, the three of them. 'Don't bother,' he told her. 'I'll get myself a drink before dinner — I had tea at the hospital. How are the lessons going?'

He was being friendly, she supposed, because Ria was there. 'The Instant English?' she said cheerfully. 'Absolutely super — the child's a wizard. Aunt Betsy is going to be very impressed.'

'I'm impressed too,' said Waldo softly, 'with your kindness and patience and affection for Ria.'

It was so unexpected that she could only stand and gape while a slow wave of colour swept over her face. 'That's a joke, isn't it?' she managed in a steady voice, 'but a cruel one after the — the things you said to me.'

She almost ran out of the room and stayed in the kitchen until Ria came in to tell her she was going to bed. They went up the stairs hand-in-hand, the little girl still chattering gaily, not noticing Olympia's silence.

She was silent during dinner too, but if Waldo noticed it he said nothing, but talked of small matters, begged her advice as to what Ria might want to do in London and asked her if she needed anything for herself.

With an effort she made herself answer cheerfully. 'No, thanks, I can't think of anything. I've bought one or two things Ria needed, and if you don't mind, I thought I might go shopping for her while we're in London – she could do with some new shoes and I want to get some Vyella for her dresses – it's cheaper there, you know.'

He smiled faintly. 'Of course, a good idea. I may have to leave you to your own devices for some of the time, but I don't suppose you will mind that.'

'You are sure you want us to come?' The question had popped out before she could stop it.

He gave her a long, unnerving look. 'Quite sure. There is someone I want you to meet – sooner than I had planned, in fact, but suddenly it's important that we . . .'

'A woman?'

She thought that for one minute he was going to laugh. Certainly his eyes were dancing, but when she looked at him, his face was grave enough. 'Yes, a woman. Olympia, there is something I must say . . .'

She interrupted him fiercely. 'There's nothing to say – there's nothing I want to know, and anyway, have you forgotten that I can't keep secrets? Whatever it is you want to tell me, I might turn it to my own advantage again, mightn't I?' Her eyes flashed and her tongue gathered speed. 'Oh, you said it was never to be spoken of again, but I can't stop my thoughts – nor, I imagine, can you.' She dug into Emma's exquisite Charlotte Russe with no regard as to its perfect shape and passed him his plate. 'You'll excuse me,' she got up rather clumsily and made for the door, 'I have a headache, I think I'll go to bed.'

She heard his urgent 'Olympia!' and ignored it as she closed the door behind her.

It was fairly simple to avoid being alone with him for the next twenty-four-hours; she had enough to keep her busy, packing and preparing for their trip, and there was Emma to confer with about the housekeeping. They met at mealtimes and if Waldo had wanted to tell her something urgent, he showed no sign of being in a hurry to do so; besides, she gave him no chance.

They travelled in the Rolls with Ria squeezed between them, to Olympia's relief, because now there would be no opportunity for Waldo to talk to her. She put a protecting arm round the child and in answer to his query, assured him that she was comfortable.

'But in England, *liefje*,' he told Ria, 'you will sit in the back and make no fuss. That is understood?'

The moppet was all obedience. 'Yes, Papa, and Mama shall sit with me.'

'Mama will sit where she is.'

'But I want her with me.'

'I want Mama too.' There was something in his voice which made Olympia look at him, meeting his eyes across Ria's head. They held an expression which she couldn't read and she made haste to say brightly:

'I'll sit here so that I can show Papa the way.' And that, she told herself, was one of the silliest remarks she could have uttered, an opinion borne out by Ria, who shrilled: 'But Papa knows the way.'

'Papa,' said the doctor gravely, 'has been getting lost lately – he has been chasing rainbows.'

Ria, highly interested, wanted to know why.

'Well, there is a song which goes: "Follow every rainbow till you find your dream" – and that is what I have been doing.'

'Did you find your dream, Papa?'

He was still staring at Olympia, who, aware of it, was scrabbling round in her handbag, her head bent. 'Yes,' he spoke slowly, 'it took me a long time, though, and even then I didn't know it at once.' He started the car. 'Have you lost something, Olympia?'

She shut her handbag with a snap. 'No – no.' Which wasn't quite true; she had a nasty feeling that she was fast losing her wits.

There was no doubting Aunt Betsy's welcome when they arrived at her house. She embraced them all in turn and then turned to Ria again, with some laughing remark in Dutch. Ria fixed her with a bright dark eye.

'I speak English,' she informed her great-aunt importantly, and having achieved her triumph, lapsed into her mother tongue. Olympia, standing a little on one side while Waldo fetched in the luggage, wasn't quite certain what she was saying, but she saw a horrified look on her hostess's face and then: 'Papa isn't my papa,' shrilled Ria, and this time Olympia understood her. 'Aunt Elisabeth told me so, but it doesn't matter . . .'

'Who told you, *liefje*?' asked the doctor from the door.

The little girl danced across to take his hand. 'Tante

Elisabeth, when she took me to the shops – she told me how I could run away to England too, she said I must because you and Mama didn't want me, but I didn't know about being your own little daughter from the day I was a baby, did I? And I didn't know Mama loved me too. Tante Elisabeth said Mama wanted me to go away, but it was a mistake, wasn't it?' She lifted her face to be kissed.

'Yes, little one, a very silly mistake. You're my daughter, and Mama's too – we couldn't be without you.' He pushed her gently towards Mrs. van der Graaf. 'Go and tell Aunt Betsy all about it. I think she will be very interested in your adventures.'

Aunt Betsy took her cue from him on the instant. 'Most interested,' she assured her listeners. 'I daresay it will take until bedtime to tell – I shall give Ria a nice little supper and put her to bed myself, and you two can go and tuck her up later.' She held out a commanding hand and with a delighted Ria in tow, swam from the hall.

Olympia watched them go, not looking at Waldo at all, although she was perfectly aware that he had shut the front door and was coming towards her. As he swung her round to face him he sounded quite shocked.

'Olympia, dear girl, why didn't you tell me?'

His hands were gentle on her shoulders, and there was something in his voice . . . she ignored it. 'I didn't know – not for certain, you see. I couldn't ask Ria because you made me promise not to speak to her about it ever again.'

'My God, I deserve to be shot . . .'

'Yes, you do,' she agreed fiercely. 'You are a most tiresome and difficult husband, and I don't think I want to be your wife any longer.' She sniffed. 'You don't believe me, and you don't tell me things . . .' She rounded on him, quite beside herself and not caring what she said any more. 'You believed Elisabeth – and now there's this girl you've come to see, and I know you only want me here so that you can arrange a divorce. Why don't you tell me that I've been a miserable failure, instead of treating me like a – a stranger? I suppose when everything is settled I'm to be told.'

He actually laughed. 'Yes, that's exactly what I had planned, but I can see that it won't do now, my pretty. There's so much I must say to you, but that must wait, there is a quicker way to explain. Now stay where you are, I have to speak to Aunt Betsy.'

He was back while she was still wondering why he had called her his pretty. He said nothing more, however, merely swept her out of the house once more and back into the car. She was composing a suitable question or two, something she could say without loss of dignity, when she noticed that they were going up Primrose Hill, and forgetting all about the dignity, she exclaimed: 'We're not going to see Aunt Maria?'

He didn't answer her, for there was hardly time, but it seemed that they were; he stopped in front of the well-remembered house and got out and came round to open her door. 'Well, here we are,' he said nicely. 'Out you get.'

'I don't think I want . . .' she began, and a long arm slid round her waist and lifted her without effort and stood her on her feet on the pavement. So much for asserting herself, she thought vexedly, and not wishing to be carried across the pavement, went meekly to the front door with him. Only as he rang the bell she protested: 'My aunt won't want to see me.'

'Your aunt isn't here,' observed Waldo blandly, and stooped to kiss her soundly as the door opened and he ushered her inside. She barely heard him say: 'It will be explained later, my darling,' – a remark, which, coming on top of the kiss, left her speechless. Mrs. Blair had opened the door, but Olympia had no time to do more than wish her good evening, for her aunt's office door had opened and a woman was coming to meet them. A rather dumpy woman, no longer young but with a merry round face, surmounted by a nicely goffered muslin cap and wearing Matron's uniform. She began to speak before she reached them, and Olympia realized with a shock that she had heard her voice before – a youthful voice, pretty and light; like a girl's – even on the telephone it had lost none of its charm.

'Doctor van der Graaf, how nice – I wasn't sure when you would – and you have brought your wife ... I wondered if ... .' She paused for breath, offered a hand and smiled largely at them both.

Waldo greeted her with easy friendliness. 'Yes, this is my wife. Olympia, this is Mrs. Doreen Betts, my dear, she and her husband run the home for me. I believe that you have already spoken to each other on the telephone.'

Olympia glanced at him. There was a gleam of amusement in his eyes, and she looked away quickly and offered a hand to Mrs. Betts, who went on chattily, 'A surprise for you, isn't it, Mrs. van der Graaf? talk about secret, and such a lot to do – everything altered and painted and papered – you've no idea. And to think that I almost let the cat out of the bag! I had no idea that day I rang up that it was you on the telephone. I daresay you wondered who I was. I hope you didn't guess?'

Olympia murmured that no, she hadn't and re-marked, feverishly, that the hall, now that it had been papered a warm red and all the paintwork a spanking white, looked delightful.

Mrs. Betts agreed with enthusiasm as she led the way to the office. 'And the whole place so bright and cheer-ful,' she went on. 'Such a busy time we've had, haven't we, Doctor? Coloured sheets and bedcovers, and easy chairs and a lift so that the top floor patients can come down to the "common" room that's been built – just like you wanted, Doctor...'

Waldo smiled at her. 'We must alter that, Mrs. Betts; it is just like my wife wanted.'

Olympia stood very still, remembering how she had opened her heart to him soon after they had met, telling him all her dreams of what she would do if she had limitless money and the chance to use it on the home – and he had remembred. Quite forgetting Mrs. Betts, she began: 'Waldo...'

She wasn't allowed to finish; he interrupted pleasantly: 'Perhaps you would like to look round, my dear, while I talk to Jim about those basement plans.'

Olympia allowed herself to be led away, to exclaim over new curtains, the central heating which had been put in, even right to the top of the house, and the pretty new furniture and comfortable wards. And so many of the old people she had known were still there, sitting round card tables – something Aunt Maria had never allowed – or reading and knitting. There seemed to be plenty of nurses too, and Miss Snow, who was on duty, assured her that Mrs. Drew and Mrs. Cooper were still there too and never wanted to leave. 'And it's to be hoped,' ended Miss Snow, rather tartly, 'that your aunt is happy in that villa in Spain.'

Olympia smiled and nodded and answered questions, all the while thinking that Spain seemed a very unlikely place for Aunt Maria to be living in; she would have to ask Waldo about it presently; she would have to ask him a great deal, but at the moment she wasn't sure what. She was quite bewildered and somewhere deep inside her there was a strong feeling of excitement. She was led back downstairs presently to meet him and listened in a bemused way while he talked about the drastic improvements there were to be in the basement, it was quite a relief when Waldo, in the nicest possible way, said that they would have to be going, and she found herself in the car once more. He had barely time to press the starter before she burst out: 'You didn't tell me about Aunt Maria.'

He gentled the car into the stream of evening traffic. 'No. I was going to surprise you.'

'You have.'

His mouth quirked in a half smile. 'Yes, but not in quite the way I had intended. I wanted to show you the home as a *fait accompli*, as nearly like your ideas as possible.

She gasped, 'You bought it?'

'Yes.' He slid to a halt by traffic lights. 'Your aunt needed very little persuasion to sell; once you had gone, she discovered that she had lost her main prop and stay.'

'Oh.' She was aware that this was an inadequate answer, but for the life of her she could think of nothing else to say. She said: 'Oh,' again before she could stop herself. She was still composing her chaotic thoughts into sensible speech when he drew up outside

Aunt Betsy's house.

In the hall she made for the stairs. She really needed
time to think, but she was not to be given it. Waldo shut
the front door behind him and leaned against it. 'No,'
he said, 'don't run away. There are things we must say,
my lovely girl.'

She stopped, her foot poised on the bottom stair.
Nobody had called her a lovely girl before. She looked
over her shoulder and saw the look on his face and
without a word turned round and walked over to
him.

'Aunt Betsy was right,' he told her, 'I should have
told you long ago.'

'What?' she asked urgently.

'A great many things, but only one of them matters.
I've fallen in love with you. You see, I found my
dream, my dearest darling, but I didn't know it, not
until Ria ran away and you went too and I thought I
had lost you.'

'But you were so angry, and you believed Elisabeth,
you didn't even . . .' He had covered the foot or two
between them in one stride. 'I deserve to be reminded
of that every day of my life,' he told her humbly, 'but
oh, my darling, it made no difference to my love for
you, can you understand that? not for one second did I
stop loving you, even while Elisabeth's logic made such
sense.' His blue eyes were very bright, staring down
into hers as he caught her in his arms. 'Oh, my dear
love, I wanted to make you happy; to do something for
you, even though I hadn't realized that it was you I
loved, and even when Ria ran away, I still wanted to
do that.'

She leaned back in his arms to look at him. 'You
should have told me about Mrs. Betts – do you know

what I thought . . . ?'

'Indeed I do, my darling, but I didn't even guess at it to begin with.' His arms tightened so that she could hardly breathe. 'Olympia, could we start again – could you learn to love me?'

She hadn't stopped looking at him; all the things she had hoped for were there now and she smiled. 'I'm not sure how you learn to love someone. I only know that I've loved you ever since that day in Middelburg when you hoped that I would be happy. I don't need to start again, Waldo.'

He kissed her then, a satisfying, lengthy operation which left her breathless, then picked her up and swung her round to set her gently on her feet again, and when she opened her mouth to protest, he kissed her once more. 'Tomorrow,' he told her, 'we're going out, you and I, and I shall buy you a gift for every day I've known you.'

Gone was the placid expression, the well-schooled calm face, his eyes held a gleam she had never seen before. There were several small problems facing them

Elisabeth, for instance, but she had the satisfying feeling that if she mentioned her by name at that moment he wouldn't even remember who she was. She reached up and kissed him. 'Waldo,' she began, and was interrupted by a small shrill voice from somewhere upstairs. She smiled. 'Your – no – our daughter, dearest.'

He grinned suddenly. 'Our eldest daughter, my darling heart.'

She kissed him again. 'It won't matter about the boys,' she mused, 'but the little girls will have to take after you.'

They began to walk, arm in arm, towards the stairs.

'My daughters,' declared the doctor positively, 'will take after their mother, although they can't hope to be half as pretty.'

A satisfying remark. Olympia, under his loving gaze, felt all at once the most beautiful girl in the whole world.

January Paperbacks

THAT SUMMER OF SURRENDER
Rebecca Caine

After her father's death Perdita's happy relationship with
Olivia, her stepmother, had brought no problems. But when
Olivia had the chance of making a new life for herself
Perdita found herself dealing with considerable difficulties—
not the least of which was the arrival on the scene of the
insufferable Blake Hadwyn!

LOVE AND LUCY BROWN
Joyce Dingwell

Lucy was delighted when a kindly lady arranged a job for
her in a hospital-cum-children's home in Australia, and
could hardly wait to get to Sydney and start her fascinating
new job. But she arrived to find herself rather less than
welcome to the doctor in charge, Tavis Walsh—and still less
to the glamorous Sister Ursula!

DARLING JENNY
Janet Dailey

Jennifer Glenn, smarting from a disastrous love affair with
Brad Stevenson, had taken herself off to the skiing grounds
of Wyoming to 'get away from it all' and lend a hand to her
busy sister Sheila at the same time. She never expected to
fall in love again almost at once—and certainly not with the
man who was in love with Sheila!

THE IMPOSSIBLE MARRIAGE
Lilian Peake

Old Mrs. Dunlopp thought it was a splendid idea to leave
her large house and a lot of money to her great-nephew
Grant Gard and her young friend Beverley Redmund—on
condition that within six months they got married. There was
one snag: the two people concerned just couldn't stand each
other!

AUTUMN CONCERTO
Rebecca Stratton

It was through the attractive young Frenchman Jacques
Delange that Ruth had lost her job, so it was really the least
that Jacques could do to find her another—working for
his uncle Hugo. But Hugo Gerard was to cause Ruth
considerably more heart-searching than his nephew!

25p net each

January Paperbacks *continued*

THE NOBLE SAVAGE
Violet Winspear

The rich, appallingly snobbish Mrs. Amy du Mont would have given almost anything to be admitted to the society of the imposing Conde Estuardo Santigardas de Reyes. But it was Mrs. du Mont's quiet, shy little companion who interested the Conde...

PROUD CITADEL
Elizabeth Hoy

Judy had burned her boats by coming out to Morocco to marry Glen Grant, against the wishes of her family. But it was another woman who was going to present the biggest threat to Judy's marriage...

WHITE HEAT
Pamela Kent

The voyage out to Australia was fun for Karin, except for the ruthlessness of Kent Willoughby—until the ship caught fire and Karin was cast adrift in the Indian Ocean with only a manservant and Kent himself.

A PAVEMENT OF PEARL
Iris Danbury

Rianna accompanied her brother to Sicily to join an underwater expedition in the hope of finding something of interest for a travel article she intended to write. But the uncompromising Holford Sinclair, leader of the expedition, made it clear that he had no time for Rianna's interference in his work. How dared he treat her like this?

HIGH-COUNTRY WIFE
Gloria Bevan

Rosanne enjoyed her work as nursery nurse aboard ship until she committed the fatal mistake of becoming too involved in the future of one of her charges, four-year-old Nicky. It was a mistake which led her into marriage with the disturbingly attractive Craig Houston, a man who felt nothing for her. Yet...

25p net each

February Paperbacks

THE SWALLOWS OF SAN FEDORA *Betty Beaty*
Air hostess Emma had enough problems to deal with—
without the uncompromising attitude of
the captain, Mark Creighton!

THE KISSING GATE *Joyce Dingwell*
'See me when you grow up,' Clem had told Silver. Now she
was grown up. Would he still be interested?

DESIGN FOR DESTINY *Sue Peters*
Jan had offered her help to Ryan St. John when he had an
accident. Now he was getting better and she could return to
her London job. But did she want to?

DANGEROUS RHAPSODY *Anne Mather*
Emma's job in the Bahamas was not as glamorous as it
seemed. For a start, there was the curious attitude of her
employer ...

THE FARAWAY BRIDE *Linden Grierson*
Janet and Neil had married for all the wrong reasons. Could
they make each other happy?

THE GILDED BUTTERFLY *Elizabeth Ashton*
Alastair Grainger had told Selina that he was not for her.
Could she accept his decision?

HEAVEN IS GENTLE *Betty Neels*
Eliza shouldn't have fallen in love with Professor van Duyl.
His Dutch girl-friend was so obviously more suitable!

FOOD FOR LOVE *Rachel Lindsay*
Amanda changed one boss for another—and one set of
problems for another, too!

THE DREAM ON THE HILL *Lilian Peake*
Nicola Dean and Connor Mitchell ought to have had a lot
in common—but in fact all they had in common was their
dislike for each other!

GATE OF THE GOLDEN GAZELLE *Dorothy Cork*
Natalie Jones had persuaded Josian Jones to change places
with her—which in Morocco was not a very sensible thing
to do!

25p net each

DID YOU MISS OUR 1974 CHRISTMAS PACK?

THE JAPANESE SCREEN
Anne Mather

Susannah met and fell in love with Fernando Cuevas in London. She little thought when she travelled to Spain to work for a wealthy family that the child she had come to teach was Fernando's child and that she would be meeting Fernando himself sooner than she had expected ...

THE GIRL AT GOLDENHAWK
Violet Winspear

Jaine was accustomed always to take back place to her aunt, a spoilt darling of the London stage, and her glamorous cousin Laraine. As it seemed only natural to *them* that Jaine should take on the difficult task of explaining to Laraine's wealthy suitor that she had changed her mind about the marriage, Jaine nerved herself to meet the arrogant Pedro de Ros Zanto. Was there a surprise in store?

PRIDE AND POWER
Anne Hampson

Leona's pride suffered a tremendous blow when she discovered that the beautiful mansion and the prosperous farm that went with it belonged not as she thought to her grandmother, but to the forbidding Konon Wyndham, a man she had always hated. Now he had the power to humble her. Would he use it?

SWEET SUNDOWN
Margaret Way

Ever since she was a little girl Gabriele had been promised a trip to Sundown, the lovely old mansion where her mother had been born. And now she was going there at last at the invitation of her glamorous aunt Camilla. What would the visit bring Gabriele in the way of a new life ... and a new love?

Available at £1.00 net per pack
either from your local bookshop or if in difficulty from
Mills & Boon Reader Service,
P.O. Box 236, 14 Sanderstead Rd.,
S. Croydon, CR2 0YG, Surrey, England.

Your copy of the Mills & Boon Magazine —
'Happy Reading'

If you enjoyed reading this MILLS & BOON romance and would
like a list of other MILLS & BOON romances available, together
with details of all future publications and special offers, why
not fill in the coupon below and you will receive, by return
and post free, your own copy of the MILLS & BOON magazine
—'*Happy Reading*'.

Not only does it list nearly 400 MILLS & BOON romances
which are available either from your local bookshop or in
case of difficulty from MILLS & BOON READER SERVICE, P.O.
BOX 236, 14 Sanderstead Road, S. Croydon, CR2 0YG,
Surrey, England, but it also includes articles on cookery
and craft, a pen-pals scheme, letters from overseas readers,
plus an exciting competition!

For those of you who can't wait to receive our catalogue
we have listed over the page a selection of current titles. This
list may include titles you have missed or had difficulty in
obtaining from your usual stockist. Just tick the selection
your require, fill in the coupon below and send the whole
page to us with your remittance including postage and
packing. We will despatch your order to you by return!

Please send me the free MILLS & BOON magazine ☐
Please send me the titles ticked ☐

I enclose £   (No C.O.D.) Please add 2p per book
for postage and packing (10p if you live outside the U.K.)

Name ....Miss/Mrs.

Address ....

City/Town ....

County/Country ....Postal/Zip Code.................

MB 12/74

Your Mills & Boon Selection

All priced at 20p. Please tick your requirements and
see over for handy order form.